T

VACATION

LODGE

D.J. WALTERS

First by published in Great Britain in 2017 by:
WW
Walters Way Publishing
www.djwalterswriter.com
djwalterswriter@gmail.com

PUBLISHER'S NOTE
This is a work of fiction. Names, characters, places and incidents are either the products of the author's imagination or are used fictitiously. Any resemblance to actual people, living or dead; events or locales are entirely coincidental.

While the author has made every effort to provide accurate contact numbers and addresses (including websites and emails) at the time of publication, neither the publisher nor the author assume any responsibility for errors, or for changes that occur after publication. Furthermore, the publisher does not have any control over and does not assume any responsibility for author or third-party websites or their content.

Catalogue record for the publication data:

ISBN-10: 199927605
ISBN-13: 978-1-9999276-0-8
The Vacation Lodge by D.J. Walters
Fiction- Romance- Erotica

Manufactured and Printed by Blurb
www.blurb.co.uk

THE VACATION LODGE

WW

WALTERS WAY PUBLISHING

For Kelly Jade;

~When I didn't, she believed that I could~

THE VACATION LODGE

~ Chapter 1 ~

Spiritless, I sat by the pool searching for an excuse to spark up a conversation with a beautiful stranger. A beautiful person. A stranger. Anyone! Booking a holiday alone seemed like such a good idea at the time, despite the harsh reality that I was actually faced with. I was on holiday, in a strange country, alone! How pathetic! The water tickled my restless feet as I challenged myself to investigate how much water I could rise into the air without dropping it. Oh, the games that my imagination conjured up when I was completely bored senseless! That was the level that I had stooped to; I had to entertain myself because I was too afraid to make the first move and start a conversation with someone else.

Most people had the pleasure of sharing their adventures with their nearest and dearest. Having someone to wake up to and hide their deathly morning breath from. They got to share an extravagant continental breakfast, too immense for one human to consume alone. Some travelled with a loyal holiday partner, who they planned wild excursions with. All I wanted was someone to have a conversation with; a basic exchange. Even a simple hello would have stimulated my intellect.

As I scanned my surroundings, I couldn't help but notice the abundance of beauty that had engulfed me. It was the polar opposite to my side of London. A forest of sky scraping palm trees marked the parameter of *The Vacation Lodge* like soldiers standing to attention. Ripe, dangling coconuts danced along the trees in the welcoming breeze. Like a warm hug, the glimmering sun embraced me, causing my skin to glow a golden brown. And the way the sun reflected off of my skin made me feel nothing short of chocolate goddess.

At home I resided in a high-rise block, south of the river, with just my father alone. Our neighbourhood was a concrete jungle located between Brixton and Peckham where everyone felt most vulnerable when they walked the streets after dark. The mean, cold faces were congruent with the English weather and I loathed talking to our neighbours, despite our close proximity in our compact building. I moved into my father's one bedroom apartment as my mother battled with manic depression. It was a dingy, small apartment located on the highest floor which occasionally became infested with rodents. He converted his living room into my bedroom so I slept right next to the kitchen. When the rodent infestations were at their worst, the noise of scuttles and scratches would keep me awake at night. Although it wasn't the most ideal situation, I found living with my father a lot more stable than not knowing whether I was going to wake up to an aggressive argument in the middle of the night or a mute mother. My father and I loved my mother dearly but neither of us knew how to manage her appropriately.

Both of my parents were born in Kingston, Jamaica and had known each other since they were in school. When they decided to move to London, they worked hard to create a more appealing future for my sister and I. My father received constant abuse from the passengers as a bus driver and my mother often worked both day and night shifts as a nurse. It was all so that we could live comfortably together. After a while, it seemed that the stresses of working extra shifts and bringing up two children had gotten the better of her; or possibly the worst and drove our small family apart. My mother had spent most of my life being carted in and out of hospitals as she tried to manage her reality. And whilst I was old enough to move in with my father, my little sister was in and out of care for most of her childhood.

As a young girl, I always looked up to my father and admired his hard work ethic. I longed to find a man that was as kind and respectful as him. I spent my days scrolling the internet to find my perfect match; my nights painting the town red in the finest of dresses and my Sunday's praising the Lord with one eye closed and the other eye on the sexy, single guys in the congregation. Despite my efforts, I struggled to find a man who was as gentle and endearing as my father and I refused to move out of his house until I did. I had been single for so long that I almost thought that there was an issue with me. I couldn't understand it. I had cocoa brown skin with thick, firm thighs. Although I held a curvy and sturdy stance, my hands and feet were elegant and petite. My thick, coily hair bounced past my shoulders and rested on my buoyant bust. Despite carrying puffy bags in the morning, almost everyone I knew commented on my bright, sparkling eyes and said that my smile lit up the room. Like my father, I strived to work hard and bring out the best in others. I didn't mean to toot my own horn but I was a catch. I wasn't quite sure what else I needed to find a decent guy.

All my friends were loved up and I was the only one left on the shelf. Since being in their relationships, they had become so boring and they never wanted to do anything that didn't involve their partners. Although none of my friends wanted to join me on holiday, I was young, sexy and looking for some fun. I had always wanted to go to Jamaica but I could never afford it. I finally had a decent job as an accountant and was desperate to treat myself.

The moment that I stepped off of the plane, it felt like I was home. The jabber of the Jamaican patois reminded me of my grandparents and the blaze of the reggae music at the airport took me back my Sunday mornings as a child. My mother would always attempt to sing along to her favourite tunes as she fried our breakfast. Everyone that I met at the hotel was so pleasant and welcoming. Although I had never experienced anything like it, it felt so right.

All morning, the intoxicating aroma from the Jerk pan had been flowing right through me, causing the insides of my stomach to do the same. Jerk! *How ironic. Or was it coincidental?* I could never tell the difference... Whatever it was, it made me feel an overflowing sense of pleasure. It was like having a mini-orgasm in my abdomen. My head bobbed carelessly as the sweet, reggae music titillated my ears. There was something about this country that just made me feel at ease. But deep inside, something still felt as though it was missing. Everywhere I looked, chatting couples surrounded me, engaged in frivolous laughter as they inhaled the fruity clouds that emerged from the depths of their electronic shisha sticks. Everyone seemed to be enjoying their time with each other.

And there I was; shades on, parked on the ledge, swivelling the last drizzle of sex left at pit of my glass. The story of my life! My cup always seemed to be left high and dry. My glass made a disorderly croaking sound as I slurped the dregs of droplets that I could I find beneath my ice cube. I had to face it; my glass was more than half empty; the well had run dry! The thirst had encompassed me. Another holiday beverage was long overdue. Sex on the beach; I definitely wouldn't have minded a helping of that; or even just another cocktail. Or just a good cock tale; an enticing adventure story to incite my despairing soul. A good book seemed like a healthy alternative to spice up my bland holiday. If I couldn't enjoy myself, at least I could through the world of the characters. I figured that following their steamy adventures could generate some creative ideas on how to cure my own drought.

"May I be of assistance?" A deep, husky voice interjected my reasoning. I flushed hot with embarrassment, somehow assuming that he could hear my thoughts. *Was he actually offering to cure my drought? That was brazen of him.*

"What do you mean?" I responded bashfully as I peered up to gain full vision of the individual who owned this deep, husky voice. It seemed as though it took a lifetime for my eyes to reach the top of his sky-scraping body. This dark, defined male had smooth, chocolate skin with slightly protruding veins that tattooed the entire length of his strapping arms. When my eyes met with his, I realised how much of a beauty he was. His teeth were so straight and so white that they made his deep set, almond eyes shine. His haircut was sharp; neatly faded close to his head complete with thick, dark eyebrows. Black, curly stubble twirled around his strong jaw line and met with his fluffy moustache. Although his face wasn't covered in hair, it was enough to travel around his bouncy lips, vaguely camouflaging his dimple and high cheek bones. I loved a strong cheek bone, especially when it was complemented with a deep dimple. My eyes fluttered as I smiled nervously at the thought that this broad-shouldered male could potentially be offering me assistance with my dry season.

"You look like you could do with another drink?" He grinned at me, revealing his bright, pearly whites. His bright smile made it crystal clear that he took good care himself; well at least his teeth for the most part.
"How could you possibly assist?" I brazenly quizzed him. Although, the statement was true, I did need a drink, I thought that I would take the opportunity to extend our exchange as it felt as though it was the first time that I had spoken all day.
"Well, it is my job of course," he stated, gesturing towards chestnut apron. My skin blushed crimson underneath my brown glow. As I looked around, I could see that he was clearly wearing the same attire as everyone else who worked behind the bar. White shirt; pristine and pressed, black trousers and low and behold; the chestnut apron. I must have been distracted by that Jamaican twang! Damn it! Not to mention his dark, chocolate skin; I didn't need to be tempted to nibble a bite out of that. Embarrassed by the thought that he was being suggestive, I awkwardly ordered another cocktail, hoping that my barefaced attempt to flirt with the bar staff would go unnoticed.

As he attended to my order, I noticed how well his trousers fitted around his buttocks. A perfect, peach print created an impression underneath his black bottoms. I thought to myself as I ogled his beauty. I certainly didn't mind him waiting on me! Expertly, he whipped up my favourite holiday beverage. He handled the glasses like pro. Tossing, flipping, whipping, twirling. It was truly impressive. My mind began to drift. I wondered whether he handled his women the same way that he handled his drinks. From the way that he fingered the pineapple chunks to the way that he used the tip of his tongue to suck on the straw and taste the flavour of my cocktail; I could tell that he had a gentle yet attentive touch. Perfectionism. If that was the way he was going to do it, I didn't mind him tasting my cocktail anytime.

He arrived with not one, but two cocktails in hand.
"Care to join me?" I giggled as he strolled over. It was a bit presumptuous of him to think that I actually wanted him to linger around but I assumed that he could tell that I was in need of some company. To be quite frank, anyone's company would have twanged my guitar and it most certainly helped that this chocolate beauty was easy on the eye.
"It's happy hour," he smirked. *Shit!* I had done it again. It was me who was being the presumptuous one. The two for one special sign waved in my peripheral, mocking my wretched attempts to inveigle some company. My tongue brushed against my inner-cheek as I flushed even hotter with humiliation. At that moment, I was truly thankful that my blush did not show through my brown skin. "I would love to but I'm working," he continued. I exhaled a sigh of relief as his response showed that I had not misread all of his signals.

"So what is a beauty like you doing sitting here all alone in sunny Jamaica?" he questioned me. I thought for a moment, unsure of my response. I considered whether it was wise for me to share with him my desperate attempt to make new friends or whether I should pretend that my friends were waiting by the bar. And then my subconscious registered his compliment. I took a moment to embrace his comment before finding an appropriate response.

"To be honest, I'm trying to figure out what's good to do around here." As I sipped my drink, I noticed his ebony eyes; they were so deep and transfixing.

"Well… What's not to do 'round here? There's always something going on day and night!" His converse sounded convincing. I guessed that he must have been an expert, considering the fact that he sounded as though he was native to the island.

"Is there anything good going on tonight?" I eagerly requested. I was desperate for some entertainment or the chance to meet new people; anything to keep me ticking over.

He quickly responded, "*The Caribbean Cove* holds an event in the evening; music, dancing, smiling; every-ting!" *Every-ting…* My eyes fluttered as his accent tickled my instrument.

"Oh, that sounds good. Are you be going there? It would be nice to see a familiar face down there." I thirstily grilled him in search of some company. And the idea of being accompanied by some rock, solid steel as I explored the island didn't hurt at all.

"I'm working until late but I'll most probably pass by afterwards." The thought alone of catching a glimpse of his lean, athletic figure sent a spark to my sex.

"Will you be there with your friends later, or will you still be alone?" It seemed as though he was either trying to find out who I was with or possibly asking me out on a date. And my intrigued brow raised towards him. Boldly, I shared with him the fact that I had travelled alone and I was looking for some fun. "Don't you worry, I'll take care of that." He shared a ballsy wink with me. Somehow, I found it unsettling. *What exactly was he planning to take care of?* I wondered.

As he left me by the poolside, I began to wonder how safe it was to go out with strangers in a strange country. My thoughts ran wild for a moment or two but I had to come to terms with it all; that was the nature of going on holiday alone. The excitement came from the risk. As I sipped my cocktail, I began to smirk at the thought of creating wild memories later on that night. I became curious about what would we do and who would we meet. And I weighed up the chances of being whisked away into the moonlight and having sex on the beach; even if it was just the drink. I was lost in my thoughts but too excited to care. I was too busy composing adventures of what could occur after dark. As I sought shade underneath a nearby parasol tree, the broad leaves cooled down my steaming hot imagination. And my thoughts turned to the spell bounding outfit that I would have to conjure up if I was in for any chance of unforgettable frolics.

~ Chapter 2 ~

Relentlessly, I fingered through the clothes in my bottomless suitcase in search of the perfect outfit to wear to *The Caribbean Cove*. I certainly didn't pack lightly. I always liked to make sure that I had enough 'just in case' outfits for any unexpected events so I had to sieve through my entire case to find something fitting. Although I was eager to find the most eye-catching piece, my attempts seemed hopeless. No matter what outfit I had tried on, I had somehow convinced myself that it wasn't good enough. They all seemed to fall in the "too category". Too tight, too frumpy, too slutty. My merciless over analytical skills had talked me out of wearing the vast majority of clothes that I had packed in my suitcase.

When I had almost given up all hope, I stumbled across my safe, little, black dress and my eyes lit up. I clutched it to my chest momentarily as I exhaled in gratefulness. I tried on the dress and began inspect myself from all angles in front of the mirror; frontwards, sideways then backwards. When I enrobed myself in that dress, it fitted like a glove. A small grin grew across one side of my face as I inspected myself in the mirror. And with the help of my infamous, black spanx, my shape looked breath-taking. They slimmed down my waist and rounded my bottom flawlessly. The dress was the perfect mix of discretion and sex appeal. The length of the all- purpose dress rose just above my knees. The long sleeves made me look respectable whilst the tight fit and the plunged neckline was the perfect show for my assets. I wore my black shoes with the gold stiletto heels to add some glimmer to my cinnamon skin. I was almost one hundred percent sure that my waiter would get the best impression of me. I was ready make a move.

Confidence oozed out of every step that I took as I strutted to the elevator like a purring lioness. My kitty-cat fluttered as the memory of his mighty wrists handling my appetizer emerged into my mind. My lioness was ready to purr even louder. A modest ping grabbed hold of my attention as the elevator doors opened wide. As soon as I stepped inside, I couldn't help but notice the sizable mirror submerged onto the back wall of the lift. Although an impressive reflection flirted back at me, I knew something was missing. I dug deep into my purse in search of my lip gloss and pulled it out speedily to ensure that my lips looked appetising. Swiftly, I slid the gloss stick across my lips. When I had finished, my lips were so shiny that the light from the elevator bounced off of them. I glowed internally as I admired my reflection in the mirror and waited for the elevator doors to open. There was no way that my look wouldn't stop Mr Cocktail in his tracks. I was finally ready to partake in the night's saga.

As I stepped out of the lift, I sought to the foyer in search of the next shuttle. I sat patiently and the clock ticked on. My fingers ran idle as I tried to seek comfort on the sofas. My feet grew cold. And despite the efforts that I had put into juicing my lips, I began licking around them nervously as I waited for the hotel shuttle to arrive and transport us to the nightclub. My mouth was now home to a thick piece of pink felt which was as dry as the Sahara desert. It had finally dawned on me that I was attempting to meet a perfect stranger in a strange country. My confidence began to wince as paranoid thoughts entered my mind. In search of some Dutch courage, I shot off to the night bar; a little tipple was sure to ease my nerves. The sweet, dark rum shot swiftly to back of my throat as I devoured it all in one gulp. It felt warm and soothing and I welcomed it with open arms.

After a few hits from the dark shots, the shuttle pulled up. A group of us gathered and formed an orderly queue as we saw it arriving. As soon as I entered, I was consumed by the booming base of the music that came from the bus speakers. My cheeks vibrated as the explosive sounds pulsed through the vehicle. I smiled to myself as I searched for a seat. I had never entered such a vibrant bus before. After I had crouched in and found a place to sit at the back, I couldn't help but sway to sounds that swept through the pint-sized shuttle. I didn't know whether it was the music or the rum, but I was definitely feeling the vibe. The bus was filled to the brim with passengers. And just as I thought there wasn't any more spaces left, the driver flipped open the arm of the chair into the aisle to create a whole new seat. My lids batted; fairly impressed by the use of space. Although, I had no seatbelt to strap me in, the squash between the window and my neighbour felt so tight that I could barely move anyway. Despite that, our bottoms still flew into the air as the driver zoomed through all of the hump-filled roads.

Finally, we arrived on the infamous strip, home to the long anticipated Cove. The hotel guests clambered off of the bus as the driver notified us all of the pick-up times. My ears pricked up as he volunteered all of the information to us; I had no doubt in my mind that I was not going to miss the last bus but I wanted to ensure that I knew all of the correct information. "The last bus will be right here at 3 am!" he hollered as the other guests shuffled to the front. Though having a curfew wasn't ideal, I made a mental note of it all. As I stepped out of the van, my eyes vigilantly scanned the streets of the unknown.

Luckily, the minibus had stopped right outside of our destination and my ears were consumed with the sounds that flowed out of the nightclub doors. The base rhythmically penetrated through my chest, causing my heart to dance in time to the hooking sounds. The streets were alive with party and the smell flavoursome food transcended through the air. But I couldn't stomach a thing. Butterflies fluttered into my stomach at the thought of how my night could turn out. A short queue formed outside The Cove. The base bounced. The crowd waited. The bouncer towered right over me. Apprehensively, I paused right outside of the club, reconsidering how safe it was to be partying alone.

"I.D. please." His forceful command wasn't one to be reckoned with and his piercing eyes coerced me into the venue.

I scanned my surroundings in search of a familiar face. I didn't even know his name. All I knew was that he was tall, lean and chocolate, with an athletic stance. His dark, full lips sprang to mind as I remembered the way he bit his lower lip in mid-conversation. Oh and his bright pearly whites. The music blazed, the people danced and the party thrived. Drinks galore. By the DJ booth, I could see a queue of people waiting desperately to receive a free swig from the midnight shots bottles. With her head tilted backwards, the MC drowned a gagging woman in two bottles of rum sours. But I decided that was all too much for me. Awkwardly, I headed towards the bar, concluding that I should order my holiday beverage; sex on the beach. Bodies bounced off of me as they bulldozed their way past the bar. Although it was frustrating, there was a small part of me that had hoped for one of the busy bodies to stop and talk so that I wouldn't feel so queer in this wild environment. So many faces mingled in the room, yet I felt so alone. Without a second thought, I shot back one drink whilst I sipped another, causing my inhibitions to slip away from me.

As I turned away from the bar, I felt a casual hand impress on the small of my waist. There he was; tie loosened; top shirt-button unfastened; Mr Ebony eyes. My cheeks began to glow. He grabbed me close, pressing his impressive piece into my pelvis. Abruptly, my heart sank into my chest, like an unhinged elevator. *What was this chocolate stranger about to do to me?* Without words, he began grinding his strong firmly onto my lady. My how strong he felt… His moves aroused my privacy. Naturally, my rhythm responded to his as we danced entwined under the night light. Our hips locked. Forwards, backwards, all around. With every move, I felt the rub of his trophy against my cloth. Right there and then, it felt as though we were the only two people in the room. I could feel his hand slowly sliding down my back as our bodies grinded in time to the rhythmic sounds. I could tell that he was trying to work his way to my derriere, but I didn't mind. He drew me in even closer with a firm squeeze a he impelled his pelvis towards mine. His male muscle flexed, feeling even firmer than before. My cave of wonders blushed in astonishment as I had never experienced a dance quite like it before. Our bodies were so in sync. His clairvoyant hips knew exactly what I wanted.

"Come with me," he demanded as he led me through the crowds with his hand. Groups separated respectfully as he coerced his way through creating an impressive walkway. He looked so mighty and swift as he commanded each space in the room. An electrocution of excitement beamed through my nerves as I grew more curious about where he was leading me to. As we continued through, it was clear that he was heading for the door. His back muscles rippled with tension and I giddily followed behind. Judiciously, the bouncer sized him up like a fierce gorilla before he allowed us to depart from the venue. They shared a few short words in what sounded like a Caribbean routine check so I stood back awaiting the grant for our departure. As we stepped through the door, he immediately wrapped a firm arm around my shoulder, and I in turn, was persuaded to place my hand behind his hardened waist. And by the feel of him, I could tell that he obviously worked hard for his body.

Although we had left the club, the party continued thriving on the streets. A rhythmic thunder of music rumbled from car speakers as bodily women boldly bounced their behinds to the beat on the bonnets of the cars. It was clear that the women enjoyed showcasing their bodies' whilst the men in turn embraced them. And as we walked along the strip, we were immersed in hollering vendors urging us to buy some of their food. Small, heavenly clouds formed around the Jerk pan, encouraging me to investigate the food with a closer inspection. Bright sparks from the glowing, hot coals char-grilled the chicken and each piece looked succulent, yet my hunger for food was non-existent. It was my sexual appetite that was ravenous. Mr Dark Chocolate held onto me firmly as he ushered me through the streets. And as we ventured further and further away from The Cove, the street got quieter, dimmer and more abandoned. He led me to an ill-lit veranda, adjacent to the restless sea. An overwhelming sense of fear launched through my veins. I felt weak. I had no idea what I had done nor what I was about to do...

He cradled my limp body into the depth of his arms, turning to face me. His ebony eyes met mine. We shared a moment. Fear transformed into anticipation. The space between us was writhe with tension. Lunging, he pounced a tender kiss on the innermost part of my neck and my heart plunged into my stomach once more. Hooking his arms around me, he repeated. Once, twice, thrice. My legs turned to jelly. Flaccid from titillation, I managed to wrap my flimsy arms around the nape of his neck in an attempt to support myself. I began to embrace the solemn darkness that surrounded us like the desert welcoming the rain. Every kiss penetrated my sex, sending an intense signal to the tip of my nerve endings. A cheeky grin warmed my cheeks as his lips brushed against my skin. My subconscious called out to me as my excitement intensified and he stroked my back with conviction.
"I... I don't even know your name..." I struggled to find words. I knew it was so wrong but it felt so right.
"Nelson baby... and I'm all yours..." His full lips rubbed against the lobe of my ear.

As his kisses got closer to my chest, he cupped the meat of my essence in the palm of his hands and my vagina fluttered in pleasure. He continued to explore my torso with his mouth. *My, oh, my...Was he ever going to come up for air?* My innermost thoughts tried to call out to me but the overwhelming sensations that were running through my body muffled my voice of reason. His gentle tongue glided down the central part of my bosom and my senses began to heighten. As his tongue got lower and lower, my body became consumed with fear. I took quick breaths as I tried to relax in the moment. But as his tongue launched over my nipple, my eyes grew wide; the beat of my heart almost jumping out of my chest. We were moving way too fast and my subconscious began to yell even louder. "I can't do this, take me back!" I grabbed his head and he froze in confusion.

"Why? What's wrong?" His puzzling eyes attempted to read through my soul.

"This isn't right. We hardly know each other." I thought I wanted this, but in reality, I was petrified. Crazy thoughts ran through my mind. I didn't know anything about him. From where he lived to what he did with his penis. I couldn't allow him to go too far. I couldn't allow myself to let go.

"It feels as though I've known you for a lifetime." His words sounded convincing but my instinct sounded even more so. The reality of my safety on the ill-lit, abandoned street had become even more apparent to me and my urge to feel safe grew stronger. I wasn't ready for him to see my vulnerability.

"It's just that I don't feel comfortable canoodling with someone who doesn't even know my name. I've never done anything like this before," I said, barely being able to pluck up the courage to lift my eyes from the floor. He slightly descended away from me with his hands in the air.
"I didn't mean frighten you, I suppose I was so caught up in your beauty that I forgot to ask you. How rude of me. What is your name by the way?" He shared an interested focus into my eyes as I looked his way.
"Raven," I muttered.
"A beautiful name for a beautiful lady." A coy smile began to appear on my face. His words were as smooth as his cocktail making skills. He made me swoon with ease but I refused to be swayed by his looks and charm; not without getting to know him.
"Thank you. Look, I'm sorry if you felt as though I was leading you on but this just seems a bit too much, too soon. I would really appreciate it if you would take me back to the club."
It was so quiet on the street that he had taken me to and I longed to feel the safety in numbers.
"You don't need to be scared with me. Your wish is my command," he spoke softly. As I gazed up, his apologetic eyes made it obvious that he was a gentle giant. He extended his hand towards mine and I clutched on to his as we strolled back towards The Cove. It seemed as though he had genuinely regretted making me feel uneasy and my fear began to subside. The closer we got to the club, the more at ease I felt.

~ Chapter 3 ~

One too many cocktails had me rising to a piercing pain like glass through my skull. My hangover encouraged my eyes to stay sealed shut, although the trickling sound of the waterfall slightly eased my suffering. I had been in and out of sleep all morning trying to recover from the midnight madness but I refused to succumb to full consciousness. The morning after never seemed as fun as the night before. And it was all too much for me to handle. Self-inflicted pains penetrated through my body whilst the warm, morning air embraced me like a quilted blanket. Lucid memories from the night before began to flood back into my mind and a modest smile began to grow on my face. I remembered the way that he clasped me so firmly whilst he dropped gentle kisses down my neck. As I laid on the sun lounger, I began to reminisce on the unforgettable dance that we'd shared. An impulsive twinge raced to my bikini line as I remembered how firm his man muscle felt against me. The thought of that alone was enough to make my flower bloom.

"That dream must be real sweet." That low, rasping voice sounded familiar. Struggling to pull my eyelids apart, I attempted to peer through my shades to address him properly. A tall refreshment with crushed ice came into vision, engulfed by a big, black hand. There was no way that I could drink any more alcohol, especially with how volatile my stomach felt.

"I think I've had enough to drink to be honest, besides…" before I could even finish, I was interrupted by his soothing command.

"Hush, it's only a mocktail. Plus, you looked parched!" He chuckled. It was Nelson. I should have known. With his strong, firm forearms and his smooth skin, he was quite different from the guys I had met before him. He exhibited a unique, quirky charm and he had a way with his words, not to mention his hands. There seemed to be power and safety behind a good pair of hands. He grinned at me from the side of his mouth, forcing both his cheek and eye to rise in unison. Momentarily, I was transfixed. "Well, are you going to drink up or not?" he quizzed me. My head was pounding and my mouth was as dry as dust so I had no option but to drain that glass. Pineapple and coconut juices briefly danced in my mouth before sliding down my throat. It tasted amazing, however, anything would have tasted just as good at the levels of dehydration I had reached.

"Thanks" I gasped.

"Thirsty much?" he mocked as he sat on the sun lounger beside me. Of course I was, especially after the images that had been floating in and out of my head all morning.

"It was a heavy night for me last night," I responded as I placed the empty glass on the table. His smile disappeared.
"I'm sorry if I made you feel uncomfortable Raven; that was not my intention," Nelson lowered his gaze as though he was disappointed in himself. And it all came flooding back to me. I had completely forgotten about how distressed I had felt at the abandoned veranda. We had so much fun afterwards; that had become a distant memory. I blamed it on the alcohol. But I knew that if it was that big of a deal, it would have made more of an impression on my memory. I didn't want to make anything awkward between us as I still had the rest of my holiday to look forward to. By default, I would be seeing him a lot more, whether I liked it or not! Although, I did like it more than I did not. Plus the look on his face caused me to feel an overwhelming sense of guilt; I was desperate to make us both feel at ease.

"I wouldn't worry too much about it to be honest. I just feel more comfortable when I get to know someone before getting too carried away! We were both drunk; it's fine." An awkward giggle sprang out of my mouth like a discarded slinky. Even though I had put my best efforts into convincing him that I felt casual about the situation, I wasn't sure that he was convinced.
"The last thing I would want to do is make you feel uneasy around me. Look, I want to take you out this evening to make it up to you and show you around a little bit. And I won't take no for an answer. I owe it to you." His fixed eyes momentarily froze my thought patterns. I was taken aback by his assertiveness.

Somehow, it had turned me on and put me in my place all at once. My cha cha danced in excitement.

"It would be nice to find out more about this country, it's a beautiful place" I smoothly stated although butterflies were back flipping in my stomach. I didn't want to seem too keen.

"Listen, I finish in work in a couple hours so we can meet by The Jerk Hut on the beach around 4 if that's cool with you," he confirmed confidently. His gaze was so intense that my soul felt naked around him. Just his look alone made me feel limp. Although I could tell that he already knew the answer, I gave him a coy smile and a nod. "I have to get back to work but I'll see you later," he told me as he rose from the seat beside me.

As he walked back through the complex, I began to smile to myself. That wakeup call was just what I needed to kick-start my mood; it had perked me up so much that my headache had almost disappeared. It was either that or the drink that he had brought me. Whatever it was, it had put me in the perfect mood for a date and I was delighted to have something to look forward to.

* * *

I decided that it would be a good idea to freshen up before I met with Nelson as it had been sweltering all day. I couldn't stand the stench of body odour so I eagerly headed for the shower. I set the temperature to cold as I stepped into the glass box. I figured that a late afternoon shower was the only thing that could purify my body and possibly my mind. Goosebumps crept all over my body as the arctic spring of water sprinkled onto my skin. There was an odd pleasure to the sensation that was felt when the water rushed over my nipples. It felt like mini, nibbling love bites all around my bosom. Momentarily, I closed my eyes and started to imagine how mind blowing it would feel to receive a thousand nipple nibbles from Nelson. My soapy hands slid down the back of my neck as I envisioned him flicking his tongue over my areola between each gentle bite. My nipples stood to attention. Inhaling deeply, my head gently began to tilt backwards like a graceful gymnast. The shower was making me wetter than I expected and clearly wasn't cold enough to cool my racing, hot imagination.

Vigorously, I rubbed the towel all over my face to bring me back to reality. I couldn't understand why my imagination was running away from me so much after I had turned him down the day before. There was something intriguing about Nelson and as much as I didn't want to move quickly with him, I couldn't shake those filthy thoughts from my psyche. As I booted one thought out, another crept in like a hungry fox in the night. The shower had caused my heart to race so much that a cold sweat began to form on my temples. As I looked myself in the mirror, I could no longer tell the difference between my own sweat and the water droplets from the shower. I was sweating more than a dirty whore in church. Wrapping the towel around me, I headed to the balcony to cool off so that I could begin getting ready for my first date.

As my body returned to normal temperature, I began to apply my makeup with a strong drink in hand. I had picked up the first thing I'd found in the mini bar that I thought would ease my nerves. Though there wasn't much to choose from, I decided to settle for the mini bottle of prosecco. A sweeping film of foam formed as I filled the glass to the brim. As I took swigs out of the glass, the bubbles bounced off of the back my throat and went straight to my head. The light fizz in my brain caused my cheeks to glow like a blushing sea on a summer's eve. My nerves subsided as the warmth of the drink ventured through my bloodstream and I was easily able to slick my hair into a neat puff. Despite my doubts, the prosecco had worked out to be quite successful.

Luckily, the sun had started set and a light breeze swept through the air, creating the perfect temperature for my flushing nerves. And as the fizz in my brain began to dull, the weather seemed to be the only thing that could deter my sweat from drenching my entire body, irrespective of the amount of deodorant I had plastered on. I was determined to play it cool; not allowing my nerves to get the better of me. So, I sought to The Jerk Hut early to mingle with the locals and deter my mind from racing.

Since I arrived before him, I ordered a light snack. I didn't know how long I was going to be there and I didn't want to look awkward whilst I waited. I made my choice quickly and it came within minutes. My eyes rejoiced in pleasure as I took my first bite. I had ordered the Jerk Lamb burger which tasted like small, tender bites of heaven. Modest slithers of lamb melted in my mouth after each soft bite; I had never tasted anything quite like it and it didn't want it to end.

Unfortunately, I had to resist the temptation of devouring the whole thing as I didn't want to look bloated in my skin-tight, denim jeans. I had tried to choose something in between dressy and casual as I had no idea where we were going or what we were doing. And I knew that my posterior looked extremely posterious in anything that was high-waisted and tight. My loose cropped top added a level of sexy discretion to my outfit; or at least that was what I had hoped for.

The mysteriousness of the date added an extra level of buzz in my cheeks and my heart was filled with anticipation. No matter how hard I tried, I couldn't seem to shift the feeling of stiffness in my thighs; it was almost as though I was stuck to the stool at the hut. I only hoped that the feeling would ease before Nelson arrived; mainly so that I could get up out of the seat but also because the tension was manipulating my thoughts. I couldn't bear to wait much longer but the time seemed to drag after I had finished my burger. For a moment, I wondered whether I was waiting in vain. I imagined how awful it would have been if he had stood me up, especially after how adamant he was to make it up to me. I desperately felt the urge to keep my hands occupied whilst I waited so I ordered myself a cocktail.

I erupted into a small spasm of silent claps when my Pina Colada arrived. Unlike the one I had by the pool earlier, this drink was no mocktail. The spark from the prosecco had started to ware off and I longed to feel the ease in my nerves once more. A small smile grew across my cheeks as I towered over my glass to inhale my first slurp.

"I could have made it better." The smooth breath from a deep whisper warmed up the back of my earlobe and I didn't even need to turn around to recognise who the whisper belonged to. The distinctive aroma from his body oozed sex appeal and I knew that there was only one person who would have the audacity to impart their breath so hungrily over my ear.

Finally, Nelson had arrived and the buzz that was in my cheeks raced down through my body and into my toes. At that moment, I sprang up to embrace him. A small giggle left my mouth as I greeted him with a faire la bise. His skin felt like velvet as his cheek momentarily rubbed against mine. It was a moment that I intended on savouring. "Are you ready to go?" he asked as he brazenly reached for my glass to slurp some of my drink. My mouth dropped in shock. I'd never had my drink slurped by a guy that I'd never shared saliva with but I took it as compliment; assuming that he didn't mind doing so. He offered his arm to me so I had no choice but to form a link with my hand through the entrance that he had made, leaving me with no time to finish my drink. I didn't mind though. In fact, my mouth had already began salivate as I clung on to him. His arms were firm and mighty and I couldn't help but brush my fingers over one solid vein that ran down his bicep. It would have been rude not to. I felt a slight clench of his arm as I handled him and his muscle doubled in size. I couldn't help but giggle internally at his subtle attempt to make an on impression me; without a doubt, it had worked.

~ Chapter 4 ~

The wet sand massaged my toes as we walked down the tidemark. We spent time chatting, laughing and actually getting to know each other. He spoke with such knowledge and it was rather pleasant see that there was actually brains behind his beauty. I loved how open he was about where he had grown up and his aspirations to create a better life for himself. It was quite amorous to talk to a guy that embraced what life had to offer whilst chasing after what he desired. I wondered whether he thought that I was worth chasing after. The more we talked, the more I could envision myself being captured by him. The time flew by as we strolled down the beach and I was enjoying every moment of it.

"Yo! Tannerman!" A voice bellowed in the distance. I noticed an energetic wave from a man reining a chestnut horse. Nelson's eyes lit up in excitement as he led us towards the man.

"Do you know him?" I quizzed. I didn't understand why a random guy was bellowing across the beachfront.

"Of course! He works at the hotel. We used to go school together too!" He beamed.
"What does Tannerman mean?" I was intrigued.
"Oh, that's just my surname... Everyone used to call me that in school," he responded.
Nelson and Raven Tannerman. I thought that my name actually complimented his. I had the habit of measuring up my name with the surname of potential suitors. I didn't mean anything by it but I believed it was a good sign of how well we matched. Although surname measurements hadn't worked out to be that beneficial for me in the past.

Nelson ushered us towards his friend and my heart started to pound heavily. I wasn't expecting to meet any of his acquaintances nor was I ready. My thought rate doubled as we neared him. I speculated on how he would introduce me or whether he would even introduce me. I didn't know whether I should speak or stand back. I didn't want to fuck things up before they had even started so I hoped that my internal monologue would guide me in the right direction. Speechless, I stood closely behind Nelson as he pounded fists with his friend and briefly caught up with him. It was as though I was his humble servant waiting to be addressed.

"So, who's your friend then?" his colleague questioned inquisitively.

"Oh, this is Raven." He gently ushered me forward. I managed to share a meek smile with him before lowering my gaze; I could never understand why I found those situations so terribly awkward. "She's staying at *The Vacation Lodge* and I promised her that I would show her around so that she could fall in love with the island and then with me." He bit his lip tenderly as he momentarily gazed into my eyes before chuckling playfully. My heart plunged into my stomach; I wasn't expecting him to say such a thing. Eyes wide, I stood gormless. I didn't know how to react to a statement like that.

"Relax, that's just how Tannerman his. Him love joke," his colleague continued, "Nice to meet you. They call me Johnson and this is Lady Diana." Johnson gestured towards the horse. As he grabbed hold of my hand, Johnson pulled me in closer to embrace me, wrapping the horse reins around my back.

Everyone I had met seemed extremely friendly in this country; that was certainly something that I was not used to. Their culture was completely different. In London, no one ever spoke to strangers ever. Whenever someone was walking along the street or on public transport, it was almost rude to even make eye contact with others, let alone speak to them. If a stranger attempted to spark up a conversation with someone else, it was the norm to think that they were weird. But on this island, it was completely different; you were almost weird if you never embraced other people. I had no choice but to accept Johnson's embrace, hoping that his four- legged friend wouldn't mind being dragged around too much. A small part of me was slightly paranoid about how the horse would react.

“Your horse is beautiful," I mentioned as I stepped away from Lady Diana. I didn’t want to continue imposing myself in her personal space although, I couldn’t help but notice how glossy her chestnut coat was. Her long, ginger mane ran all the way from the tip of her forehead to the bottom of her neck. Though my knowledge on horses was not that extensive, I had never seen a horse quite like her; she was mesmerising.
“So why don’t you treat your friend to a likkle ride down the beach?” Johnson turned to Nelson, offering him the reins of the horse. While his eyes beamed at me in excitement, I wasn’t sure if I was capable of sharing the same reaction. My eyes widened but in fear rather than excitement. I had never even been near a horse a day in my life, let alone riding one along the beach. I held my breath involuntarily.

“Don’t worry, I’ll take care of you," Nelson assured me, almost sensing my fear. Nelson winked as he grasped the reins of Lady Diana; he definitely knew how to take control.

Without hesitation, he jumped up and wrapped his legs firmly around the equine. Lady Di jolted forward but he gently reined her back. He offered his hand down towards me for support as I clambered onto the horse, not quite as elegantly as he did. At that moment, I became grateful for my decision to wear jeans that day, though my sandals weren't quite as fitting. But Johnson didn't seem to mind; he was probably used to the idea of people riding his horse in beach wear. After I had managed to comfortably sit on top of the horse, Nelson grabbed hold of my hands and wrapped them around his midsection. Gripping onto him tightly, I could feel his sturdy abdominals bulging through his shirt. My eyes gleamed in pleasure behind him. He had more core than an apple and I certainly didn't mind grabbing hold of it.

As we galloped off down the beach, I leaned forward with an even tighter grip to prevent myself from falling. I cradled my head on top of Nelson's shoulder so that I could see the view. The wind blew in our faces as we hurtled over the rocks but I didn't care; it was a brilliant way to see Jamaica. My bottom bounced up and down on the saddle whilst my breast rubbed against his back; what a thrilling ride. Being up on that horse gave us such a panoramic view of the ocean. The waves crashed furiously as the sun caressed the clouds. It was such a beautiful sight to witness. Although we were moving so fast, the view was so captivating that it felt as though everything was happening in slow motion. The waft from the seaweed began to strengthen as Lady Diana's hooves collided with the tide. Although the stench was undesirable, it didn't seem to matter because I was learning so much in such a short space of time. In the distance, I could see an abundance of mountainous greenery that was so tall that it almost kissed the clouds. As we rode, Nelson told me ancient stories about all of the runaway slaves that had retreated to the mountains. I was captivated by his words as he shared the almost hidden history of the island. And immediately, I felt a sense of pride by getting a better understanding of some of the achievements that my ancestors had faced. It was most definitely uplifting.

The hollering of the local venders interrupted our discourse as they advertised all of the tropical fruits that they wanted to sell to us. I had never tried any authentic Caribbean fruits before and they never served anything like it in *The Vacation Lodge*. He proudly waved the guineps in the air like a patriotic flag and it made me even more intrigued to find out why he took such pride in his fruit. There was something appealing about trying new experiences and I most certainly didn't want to miss out on this one. Fortunately, I was able convince Nelson to stop and speak to the vendor so that I could try some of the fruit for a local price. After bartering for a short while, they came to a mutual understanding and he was able to get the fruit for a good deal. His assertive bartering techniques were extremely impressive and something that I could get used to. Nelson was not backwards in coming forward and never seemed to shy away from a challenge. To be quite frank, his decision making skills were actually quite sexy.

Shortly after Nelson had dealt with the vendor, we found a quiet spot to retreat to as I explored my new discovery. We tied chestnut Diana to a sturdy tree whilst we rested for a while underneath the shade. My attempt to eat the guinep was challenging at first. The tough, green shell was so hard to penetrate that I had to use my teeth to pierce the skin and sample the fruit. The juice squirted rapidly out of the shell and dripped down my fingers like a sweet, oozing sap. It reminded me of a smooth-skinned Lychee. And when I put the fruit into my mouth, it felt as though I was sucking on sweet and sour cotton ball with a seed the size of a gobstopper. Although it was quite an odd sensation, the acquired taste and the challenge of the guinep became quickly addictive and before I knew it, I had finished the whole bunch. And though I felt a little greedy, I was glad that I tasted that discovery.

"Won't Johnson be worried about Lady Di?" I questioned in a concerned manner. We had been missing for quite some time and I didn't want to take advantage of his generosity.
"No. He's fine. I've known him for too long for him to think that I would run off with his horse. Besides, I can hardly hide her from him anyway!" he mocked as he gestured to the size of the horse and I laughed along at his corn-filled joke. "If you are that worried, you can ride the horse back to him," he suggested.
"Me?" My brows rose upwards in shock. There was no way I could manage that horse all the way along the coastline; I could barely manage to hang on at the back of the horse.
"Don't worry, we can take it slow. Also, you have a dedicated teacher with you so if you fall, it'll be my pleasure to catch you."

He chuckled. His banter was endearing and had somehow convinced me to attempt to ride back to his friend, with his support.

My heart pounded heavily as I attempted to take first seat on the saddle. Nelson placed a gentle but firm hand on my waist to support me as I tried to mount her. Although I momentarily lost my balance, I was able to successfully climb onto her back. It was the first time that I actually had the opportunity to touch Lady Di and the stroke of her glossy coat felt so velvet soft that I was taken aback. Although she looked healthy, I didn't expect her to feel that smooth. A fierce jolt interrupted our moment as Nelson straddled the horse. He smoothly slid his hands over mines as he placed the reins in my hands. I gripped onto them so tightly that my hands burned hot. "Don't worry, we can start off together," he assured me. As he moved closer to me, I could feel his third leg stroking my lower back. The hot flush ran from my hands, down my back and into my underwear; with the ride becoming more thrilling than I had expected.

After getting off to a bumpy start, I began to grow in confidence as I straddled the horse back down the beach. We rocked back and forth as we guided the direction of the chestnut, brown beauty. I actually felt like I was starting to fall in love with Lady Di; the way she gracefully carried us was fascinating to watch. I was in awe. I couldn't actually believe that I was riding a horse and I was in control! Nelson's thumbs began to stroke the small of my back as he let go of the reins and held onto my waist. My mouth began to dry up as he smoothed his fingers along the bottom of my midriff. A sensational throbbing begun down below and I tried desperately to ignore it. As a distraction, I decided spark up a conversation about horses in Jamaica but the touch of his hands on my skin was hard to disregard. And although his intellect was compelling, I yearned to be pulled even deeper into his field.

It was not long before we had arrived back to Johnson and an overwhelming sense of sadness came over me. I was not ready to leave Lady Diana and I most certainly wasn't ready for our date to be over. Eventually, I managed to climb off the horse and I gave her a gentle stroke goodbye. Climbing off was easy in comparison to bidding an adieu. It seemed as though I had developed quite a deep attachment to her in such a small space of time, though that was quite usual for me. I was truly grateful for the horse ride as it allowed me to discover so much so quickly; about Jamaica, horses and of course Nelson. Without Lady Di, I didn't know whether we would have had that same opportunity.

* * *

As we strolled along the beach, we found two abandoned deck chairs and thought that we would use it as an opportunity to rest our tired bones. Nelson moved his chair closer to mine and parked himself on to it with one arm resting behind his head so that he could look up. It felt like heaven to actually have the opportunity to lay down for a while as it had been such an exhausting evening. The sun had started to set and everyone had begun to desert the beach yet, I wanted to stay. It looked beautiful to see the sea illuminate in red as the sun kissed the horizon.

“I’ve really enjoyed our evening," I shared as I glanced over to Nelson. His bulging bicep forced his T-shirt to slide up his arm; his gun looked loaded and ready to blow. I didn’t know what to expect when I stepped off of the plane but I was beginning to love every moment of it.

“It’s been a beautiful time with a beautiful person and I mean that Raven.” My cheeks began to vibrate as he gazed intensely into my eyes and then to my lips.

The space between us writhe with tension. I had to fight so hard to resist the temptation to lurch forward but his plump, juicy lips looked so inviting. My mouth began to swim with saliva as he leaned towards me and I couldn’t help but gulp it down so that my tongue had enough space to breathe. I knew that he was coming for me and the throb in my underwear had come back with a vengeance. As he leaned forward, his nose began to stroke mine and I couldn’t help but inhale the deepest of breaths. His skin smelt irresistible and it reminded me of spicy cinnamon. Although I was desperate not to make the first move, my head began to rise involuntarily as he pressed his lips against mine. I felt a rush of energy shoot straight to the tip of my lady garden.

Flowers bloomed below as his tongue danced with mine. As he continued, he swiftly slid his hand down my waist and drew his hips closer to mine. His girthy stick made an impression on my lady; feeling solid as a rock. His eyes glittered momentarily as he gave me a cheeky smirk underneath the parasol. That look was so mesmerising that it made my heart melt. As our kissing intensified, he couldn't resist climbing on top of me and intertwining his legs with mine. His chest warmed mine as they rubbed against each other and the friction caused my nipples to stand firm.

Anxiously, I attempted to scan our environment as he planted tender kisses onto my chest. We were in such an open space yet it felt as though we were in a world of our own. My hairs stood on end as he nuzzled my crop top upwards. I felt a sense of mischief as he slipped his finger underneath my bra to expose my nipple. I had never done anything like it before. I had never dreamed of exposing myself in such an accessible environment but it felt so right. The more he kissed, the deeper he inhaled my scent. My chest rose towards him, lusting for him to plant his lips deeper into my bosom. And he responded with pleasure. He began to stroke his tongue swiftly over my nipple as he groped the circumference of my breast. And my hands explored his firm back as he nuzzled his face in between my squeezed bust. My head swirled as he lapped both of my nipple tips simultaneously like a dog thirsty for water and my pants began to soak. My pelvis gravitated upwards as his tongue swirled down my stomach. I wanted full penetration there and then but my subconscious was petrified of being caught by a passer-by.

"We can't..." I mustered as I grabbed hold of his head. Words that I didn't want to leave my mouth but thought that I ought to say.
"Don't worry, no one is here. Trust me," he mumbled as he slowly kissed along the waist of my jeans. *Don't worry...* they seemed to be his favourite words. I couldn't tell whether he was saying those words so that he could get his wicked way with me or because he knew that we were safe. But admittedly, he was right; I did spend too much time worrying and it sometimes got in the way of me letting loose. Whatever the reason, his kisses were so hard to resist that it had convinced me to go a little further. His nose nuzzled deeply into my navel as if he was desperately searching for gold. Each kiss grew more intense as he lowered down my body and his tongue began to stroke the top of my pelvic line in between each one.

He began to unbutton my jeans and unzip them with his teeth. I inhaled deeply as he traced his tongue from my belly button right up to my nape of my neck. With every trace, he swirled his tongue in varying directions as if he was working his way through a mysterious maze. He caressed my neck with his mouth as he rhythmically circled his fingers on top of the crutch of my underwear. The heat from his warm breath lingered on my collar bone like a steaming sauna. The more he circled his fingers, the larger my clitoris grew. I wanted more of him so I began to slide my hands down the back of his linen trousers to grope his firm buttocks. At that point, I eased his trousers down from his waist then pulled him closer to me. My heart pounded as he rested his stiff piece on the entrance of my dome. After pulling my jeans completely down to the ground, he began to grind on me so hard that my lady lips slipped through the side of my knickers. My hips moved in time with his as his third leg burrowed in between mine.

My mouth began to moisten as his tip kissed around the entrance of my base. My door began to widen as his bell continued to press into me. No matter how hard my mind tried to fight it, my body was ready to welcome him in. Surges of anticipation shot through my body as the tip of his bell entered my dome. He began to thrust his way into the depths of my vagina. Each time, plunging deeper, deeper and deeper. With every stroke, it felt as though he was thrusting my elevator further and further upwards to the top floor and there was nothing that could stop him; I didn't want to either. His hips gyrated as his tool explored every nook and cranny inside of me. My hips responded to his as he circled the walls of my precious home. It was as though his penis was searching for something sacred but whatever he was looking for, it was my pleasure to help him find it. Our lips rubbed furiously against each other's as he began to thrust harder, harder and harder. My instrument began to swell; it felt as though I was about to explode. He cupped his hands underneath the pads of my shoulders as he continued to drive his way deeper into me.

More and more tingles rushed around my face as his mallet pounded my g-spot over, over and over. It was too much. An overwhelming vibration of pleasure took possession of my body as he took possession of mine. With each hit, he added more power and a gush of ecstasy pulsated out of us. One final stroke caused him to shudder uncontrollably before he collapsed into my arms. I grinned from ear to ear; there was nothing that could erase that smile from my face at that moment. We laid there still for a while as he clasped on to me, relishing the moment and taking it all in. It was my first real taste of sex on the beach and we were exhausted.

We laid there so long that we had been witness to the sky transform from a deep indigo to a pitch black. The sky was covered in a sheet of darkness and the evening breeze had mutated into a night chill. My hairs began to raise on end as goose bumps sprouted all over my body.

Although, I didn't want the evening to end, I knew it was time to go as his body heat was no longer keeping me warm and I was wearing practically next to nothing. We decided to get dressed and head back to *The Vacation Lodge*. He wrapped his arm around me as we strolled back along the beach. Even though I was in an unfamiliar place, his embrace made me feel so safe. I had appreciated every experience of the night and did not regret one part. Every moment had happened just as it was meant to; at the right place and the right time. We shared a lingering kiss at the front gates before departing from one another. I didn't want him to leave, but I knew that he couldn't stay; it was hotel policy. That part was out of my control.

My mind couldn't help but reminisce on the night's events as I clambered into my sheets. With every image came a lucid sensation; it felt as though I was reliving every moment of a beautiful dream. I had been laying on my side fantasizing so long that I had lost the feeling in left arm. Slowly, I rolled over onto my back in order to regain sensitivity and eliminate the prickly sensation from the left side of my body. I contemplated whether I was on his mind just as much as he was on mine. At that moment, I picked up my phone to search for his number in my phone book. He looked so delicious in his display picture; I ogled at it for a while admiring his chocolate, button nipples and rippling abdominals as he posed by the edge of the West End Cliffs. Fearless indeed. I couldn't resist pressing the green button to hear his sweet voice once more before the night ended. My heart pounded as his phone began to ring. With each ring my heartbeat pounded stronger and stronger. There was a pause.

"Good night?" A polite voice answered the phone but it wasn't Nelson's. I grew worried as I hadn't heard from him since I had been back. A million thoughts whizzed through my mind. *Was he hurt? Did he get home? Was he safe?*

"Hello, is Nelson available?" I responded just as politely. I leant forward, eagerly awaiting a response that would put my mind at ease.

"Nelson is in the shower right now but you are speaking to Mrs Tannerman, his wife. Is there anything that I can help you with?" My heart stopped beating and plunged deep into my chest. *His wife?* I found it hard to believe. The way he gazed into my eyes and touched me so passionately, there was no way he could possibly have a wife. *But why would she lie?* "Hello? Are you still there?" The lady's voice interrupted my thoughts. Though my mind was full of questions, there were none that she could answer.

"Sorry. Hi, I am still here. Thank you but I will call back at a later time. Goodnight. " I replied putting on my most professional of voices. Whilst I was curious, I didn't want to disrupt her evening or cause her to be concerned. Home wrecking was not my forte.

For a while, I stared into space as my mouth clamped open. I refused to believe that I had spoken to Nelson's wife. He looked too young to even have a girlfriend let alone a wife. There was no way Nelson was ready to settle down with a family. His actions from the evening were proof of that alone. As I laid there, a deep wrinkle compressed my eyebrows toward each other; I was seriously confused. *His Wife? This has to be some sort of sick joke!* I tried to convince myself but my attempts were weak. Bemused by my thoughts and his actions, I buried my head deep into the pillow and covered my entire body with the bedsheets. I hoped that a goodnight's sleep would help clear my mind.

~ Chapter 5 ~

Time stood still as I laid motionless in my bed, glaring at the ceiling. A thick layer of water began to glaze over my eyes and blur my vision as I wandered deeper into my clouded thoughts. The morning sun crept through my open curtains like an innocent, wandering child in search of a friend. Flashes of light flickered through the television screen whilst the sounds of the daily news droned through my ears but I couldn't care less. I was more concerned about understanding what had happened before I fell asleep. My eyes carefully followed my thoughts as I struggled to retrace the events of the night before; it all appeared to be a fuzzy dream. It just didn't make sense. In search of some clarity, I reached over towards the bedside table for my phone and examined my recent calls and messages. There it was; last call dialled: Nelson Tannerman. That was all the confirmation I needed. My fingers rubbed briskly across my forehead then my eyelids. *It couldn't be.* My mind began to race as it dawned on me.

My gut hurtled up towards my throat as I imagined Nelson subduing his wife like he did with me. The nausea worsened when images of him fucking his wife after he had just fucked me swarmed into my head like swooping bees attacking my sanity. The longer I thought about it, the harder it was to rationalise the conversation that I had with that woman the night before. I was desperate to shake that awful feeling. Impulsively, I threw back the covers and headed for the bathroom. I caught a glimpse of myself in the mirror. What a mess! Smeared makeup smudged all underneath my eyelids like a beaten panda bear. I was so exhausted from over thinking the night before that I hadn't even mustered up the energy to wash my face before I had fallen asleep. As I stared in the mirror, I shook my head in disappointment at the fact that a guy that I had known for all of two minutes had me feeling so lousy.

Streams of water raced into the bath and pounded against the bottom as I twisted the tap to fill the rounded, porcelain tub. Plugging the water, I began to pour in an entire bottle of the hotel *Aromatic bubble bath.* The more I poured, the duller the sound of splashing water got as mountains of bubbles formed a sheet on top like a steamy cotton field. One foot, then two, I de-robed and slid in. An overwhelming sense of relief departed from me as I sunk in deeper. A long bubble bath was just what the doctor had ordered. The longer I laid there, the more my anxiety dissolved away into the water.

A powerful vibration from my phone interrupted my serenity. Strings of water dripped off of my arm as I reached for my phone.

"Good morning my beautiful, black bird," the message read. It was Nelson. I couldn't help but roll my eyes in frustration as I slammed my phone back onto the table. I couldn't believe the cheek of him to text me whilst he was probably laying in bed beside his wife. My paranoid thoughts had gotten the better of me. A pulse began to strengthen in my stomach as my breathing intensified. And my blood began to boil. I splashed hot water onto my face as an attempt to calm my intensifying mood. Fear had transformed into anger. Torn between the urge to block his number and aggressively fill his inbox with profanities, I decided to ignore his weak attempts to continue to woo me. Besides, I refused allow his presence to unsettle my chi. Plunging backwards, I placed a hot flannel over my eyes in order to re-enter my zone of relaxation.

Another buzz, followed by another then another. The persistent vibrations coerced me to pick up my phone once again to find out what was so urgent.

"Raven? Are you there?"

"I couldn't get you off of my mind last night,"

"When can we meet again?" I laid there frozen momentarily, confused by his brazen attempts to continue a conversation with me despite his previous message being read and ignored. *How dare he still try and pursue me?* I was convinced that he must have spoken

to his wife or whoever answered the phone after he came out of the shower the night before.

"?" He sent a single question mark. It was clear that he was waiting for some sort of response. I briefly contemplated whether I should give him the pleasure of speaking to me again. A small part of me wondered why he was so persistent in continuing to know me. I was bound by the fact that I was sure to bump into him again on the hotel complex.

"I think we need to talk," I began to type. I couldn't stand the thought of having awkward passings in the hallways for the rest of my stay at *The Vacation Lodge*. I thought it was better to be amicable with someone who had shared such an intimate part of me rather than blatantly ignore them for the rest of my holiday.

"I'd love to talk and more," he wrote back and my eyebrows buried themselves into my forehead. There had to be a valid reason for his continuing attempts to pursue this situation. It was clear that there was a misunderstanding between us that needed to be ironed out.

"Meet me at the Sports Bar at 6," I blankly replied. There was no way that I could entertain flirtation from a taken man. I had jumped into the driver's seat to take control. He began typing then stopped. He began typing again…

"I can't wait to see you then." One brow raised in suspicion so I replied with a simple thumbs up. I was determined to get to the bottom of this situation, face to face.

My toes began to shrivel into raisins as my steaming bath grew cold, so I decided to pull the plug. Soaking wet, I carefully stepped out of the bath before the water rapidly swirled down the drain. It was not in my nature to get myself intertwined in the middle of whirling mess; I preferred to get out before things got too deep. Wrapping the towel firmly around me, I began to cultivate a fool-proof action plan that would deter me from accidentally bumping into Nelson in the hallways of the complex. I had no intentions of seeing Nelson without having time to compose all of the questions that had been racing through my mind.

Without hesitation, I rummaged through my suitcase to find suitable beach attire. Being by the sea always made me feel at one and allowed me to digest and accept my thoughts. As I scrambled through my suitcase, I found my loyal beach bag and began packing it with the necessities needed to escape for the day. Rose-gold mirrored shades so that no one would be able to see where I was looking; a note pad and pen for my thoughts; a long shawl to cover me in the case of a waft of wind; a large, floppy beach hat to protect me from the sun and ogling eyes; a towel and a huge bottle of water to keep my thirst at bay. Getaway bag packed and bikini ready, I headed for the beach. I lowered the brim of my hat as I headed towards the stairs in an attempt to ensure that I looked inconspicuous. I wasn't entirely sure whether my overflowing hat and mirrored shades would detract or indeed attract more attention to me but I was willing to give it a go.

Unaware of Nelson's whereabouts, I paced through the complex and onto the beach in search of a lonesome deckchair and parasol.

* * *

The beach was brimming with holiday makers romping in the sea and toasting their precious skin in the sun. Children were occupied either burying their parents deep into the sand or attempting to build sandcastles that competed with the height of their body. Families joyfully jumped over the waves as they crashed against the seabed, followed by an insurgent splutter of laughter. Whilst everyone seemed to enjoy their carefree frolics on the beach, I was focused on finding a suitable place to rest my feet and my mind. In the distance, I spotted a shaded deck chair by the beach bar and I immediately sought comfort on that seat. Pad ready, I proceeded in pouring out my soul onto the piece of paper. The motion of the pen in my hand gave me a sense of control over my thoughts. Each word made me feel more at ease and gave me a clearer understanding of where I wanted my talk with Nelson to lead.

"Looks like you're writing a good book there." A voice chuckled as it neared me. "Can I read some?" His converse had intruded on my reasoning. My eyes rolled back into my head as I searched for the words to finish my sentence.

"Don't you know that it's rude to interrupt a woman when she's writing?" I was in no mood to entertain general chit chat as I had a lot to get off of my chest.

"You're a feisty one aren't you? I never did like to turn down a good challenge." As I peered up, a deep dimple with a gapped tooth came into my line of vision as this cute looking stranger smirked back at me. It was the last thing I expected or needed for that matter. Nelson had already tarnished my idea of Jamaican men for being swaave and sneaky but I couldn't deny that this guy was cute. He wore a blue and white uniform with snug shorts which barely covered his protruding quads. He was slightly chunkier than my usual type but his well-marked six pack made it clear that he took great pride in his body. His tightly braided dreadlocks were neatly packed into a ponytail and dangled so far down his back that they almost stroked his bottom. He wore studs in both of his ears which complemented his piercing, hazel eyes and his sun-kissed, caramel complexion. His naturally highlighted hair was the most unusual cinnamon colour and his thick golden-stroked eyebrows matched his lengthy goatee. He was something different. I had never laid eyes on anyone like him before.

"Junior Hamilton. What's your name pretty lady?" he exclaimed as he extended his hand towards me. An involuntary eyebrow raised in suspicion at the fact that I had heard a similar line before.

"My name is Raven and to what do I owe the pleasure?" I chuckled internally, intrigued to see what story he would muster up as an excuse of conversing with me.

"I would never dare to walk past a woman who possesses such beauty and the fact that I caught you writing fascinated me even more. You are clearly a woman of intellect." *Wow. He articulated that well.* He sounded like a writer himself.

"Oh, really? And what book did you read that in?" I simpered. There was no way that he could convince me that he came up with that idea by himself.

"None. I only speak what I see. Honesty is my policy. Do you care to share some of your writing with me?" he asked as he parked himself onto my deckchair. My eyelids widened with fear behind my rose-tinted glasses. Automatically, I slammed my notepad shut in embarrassment at the thought that this caramel cutie would've caught a glimpse of me pouring out my heart to a married guy that I barely knew.

"Private matters of the heart," I mumbled as I sat up right to make space for the two of us on the chair.

"Really now? You know the best love songs come from private matters of the heart. I'm a lifeguard by day and a singer by night." My ears and nipples stood to attention. The thought of a soulful singer serenading me made me weak at the knees. "I would love for you to come and see me perform tonight," he continued. I paused. I was unsure whether he was asking me on a date or promoting his gig, but either way I was sceptical. Musicians were

known to be friendly with the weaker sex and the thought of him performing was already making me feel that way.
“I’m not sure if I’m comfortable going to one of your gigs alone." I began to gnaw on my fingernails. Whilst I wanted to keep my options open, I was unsure how the conversation with Nelson would end in the evening.
“Don’t worry, if you come with me, you’ll be in safe hands." *Don’t worry;* those famous words. They would’ve fitted perfectly in the Jamaican anthem.
“I can come and pick you up at 10 if you'd like?” I pondered momentarily. I'd never been shown this much attention in such a short space of time but I never did like to put all of my eggs into one basket.
“Listen, I’ll take your number and have a think about it. If it sounds good then I’ll contact you this evening." If I met him at 10, it would allow me time to clear things up with Nelson and move forward accordingly. I pulled out my phone and waited patiently for him to relay his number.
“That sounds like a plan," he agreed as he leant over me to dial his number into my phone.
“Let me not stop your writing. I’ll look forward to hearing from you later." He shared a brief smirk with me before walking off along the beachfront. I wasn’t sure how the night would end but the mystery of it all excited me even more.

~ Chapter 6 ~

Over and over again, I read through the notes that I had made earlier on that day so that I could be clear on exactly what I thought and what I wanted to say to Nelson. It was almost as though I was revising for the most important exam of my life. I held the conversation with such high importance and I wanted to ensure that everything I thought was covered. As I continued to re-read my thoughts, one sentence stood more prominent than the others. *Why would you sleep with me if you have a wife?* It intrigued me the most. Whilst I was sure that I was an attractive female with magic melanin, I couldn't get my head around why he would opt to pursue me, to the point of full penetration, knowing that he had a wife waiting for him at home.

Although the dim lights made it harder for me to read as I entered the Sports Bar, it made me feel very comfortable in there; I had a sense of anonymity. A hue of mist drifted through the room aimlessly. There was something mellowing about being in the Sports Bar. No one seemed to bother anyone apart from the people that they came with. Small groups of people huddled at high tables in private corners as they chattered over drinks. Some stood civilly and some sat on stools.

A little smoker's corner had begun to emerge on the back deck as the nicotine fiends followed the puffs of smoke that germinated in the air. Cigarette sticks glowed brightly as the smokers inhaled each pull deep into their lungs. I never quite understood the joy that people got from inhaling smoke and I couldn't stand the smell of it either. I occupied a cosy armchair and put my shawl on another to present the chair as taken. A taken chair for a taken man. My lip curled intensely at the thought of it. Pool shots fired sharply across the cotton, blue table as friends competed against each other to pot all of their balls first. Onlookers gathered around as the men paraded around the ill-lit table following their rolling balls. That was something that the men here seemed to be very good at; following wherever their balls would take them.

In the distance, I could see Nelson waltzing through the double glass doors so I quickly smuggled my note pad into my leather hand bag. He briefly scanned the venue. I signalled. He walked over with a glimmer in his eyes. My heart pounded and my lips clasped firmly.

"Hi, it's so good to see you again!" he exclaimed as he leaned towards me for an embrace. My arm stayed fused across my

bosoms. He paused and stepped back. "Are you okay?" he asked as he attempted to cross-read my eyes. I gave nothing away.
"Well, actually no. Not entirely. I had an interesting phone conversation yesterday…" I paused to scorn him intensely but he looked back at me with a blank expression as though he hadn't a clue what I was talking about. "With Mrs Tannerman, your wife?" I continued. I read his expression as his eyebrows began to rise towards his hairline. I waited patiently for his response as I longed for him to tell me that I had been mistaken.
"My wife?" he questioned as he narrowly eyeballed our surroundings once more.
"Yes. I called your phone to speak to you but she said you were in the shower?" My heart clenched tightly as I urged for him to deny it all.
"Oh, that's weird…" My heart began to glow as he spoke. "She never mentioned that anyone called." My fingers grew cold as I felt my heart plunge into my gut.
"So it's true. You do have a wife?" I quizzed him fiercely. I was so disappointed that he had conveniently forgotten to mention the fact that he had a wife before he slipped his dick into my vagina.
"Yes. I am married but…" He halted. I leaned forward in the hope to hear news that would enlighten my soul once more. I needed to hear anything that could explain his infidelity. They were separated, unhappy or that she was dying from some incurable disease. "We have an open marriage that works for us," he humbly shared. A nauseous feeling began to erupt in my

stomach but I was determined to have all of my questions answered.

"Why would you sleep with me if you are happy with your wife?" I finally shared my undying question. I was totally bemused by his honesty.

"I've known my wife all of my life but she is aware of my needs and the industry I work in, so she doesn't mind if I get intimate with other girls, as long as I meet her needs," he brazenly explained. I was still focused on the fact that he mentioned his industry. He was behaving as if he worked in strip club, not a hotel. My lips began to pierce deep lines below my cheeks.

"Did you not feel the need to tell me this before we had sex?" My feeling of disgust intensified.

"I wanted to tell you but I didn't want to spoil the moment as I know that it can be off-putting for some people," he responded apologetically. A single eyebrow raised towards my forehead. Off-putting indeed.

"I wanted you to get to know me first then understand my situation." He glanced towards me with a solemn look in his eyes.

"I don't sleep with married men." My eyes began to fill up at the thought of me compromising my morals for a man that belonged to another.

"My wife doesn't know who I am sleeping with but she does know that it can happen from time to time. What happens between us is between us." He extended his palm up and towards me in a bargaining fashion. However, his bargain appeared one sided as I was bound to end up with the short end of the stick.

"Are you actually being serious right now? You have to be taking the piss." I needed confirmation. What he was coming out with was so absurd that there was no way that it could be true.
"Yes. Girls do this sort of thing all the time. It's no big deal." He tried to shrug off my concerns. "Vacations are all about having fun…" But his words made my blood run cold.
"I'm sorry Nelson but I think I've heard enough."
"Oh, don't be a spoil sport. We were just starting to have fun..." he smiled but I couldn't return the favour.
"No, it's not my style. Thanks but no thanks," I snapped as I shot out of the chair and declined his offer.

I was taken aback by how casual he was about the idea of cheating on his wife. I pondered for a moment on whether he thought that it was acceptable for her to do the same whilst I headed for the exit. However it was that they conducted their relationship, I wanted to have no part in it and I was desperate to get away from it all. But as the glass doors closed behind me, I noticed a pining look in his eyes which followed me until I had disappeared from view in the lobby. Briefly, I gave him a second thought then quickly convinced myself otherwise. Although his pining eyes had haunted my psyche, I knew it was the right thing to do.

For my entire journey back to my room, I couldn't shake the idea of him sleeping with me then his wife. Blood boiled in my veins as I paced down the hallways. I didn't understand how she could be okay with it all. My lips pursed at the thought of me sharing

Nelson with someone else, let alone my husband. I burst through the door then face forward, I collapsed onto my bed like a house of cards. Absolutely devastated. My fantasies with Nelson had been crushed and splattered across the room like a bunch of stomped tomatoes. I laid still for a moment as a forceful exhale left my lungs in search of a pick-me-up.

My eyes were drawn to the mini bar as it whispered my name. When I opened the fridge door, the lack of option was striking. A can of coke, a sprite, a small bottle of rum and a vodka. I thought carefully for a moment to take in the abundance of "choice" that I had. A short glass of rum and coke on the rocks was sure to lighten my mood. I smirked internally as I proceeded to fill my glass with 3 parts rum and 1 part coke. I sipped slowly as I searched for an entertaining show on the television. As I flicked through frivolously, nothing seemed to hold my interest. My phone began to ring. I peered over. It was Nelson. My eyes wound so far backwards into my head that I could see last Wednesday; the moment when we had first met. So much had changed in such a short space of time. Not quite brave enough to reject the call, I decided to let it ring out. Then it proceeded to ring once more. He was quite persistent. It seemed as though he had got into the awful habit of continually ringing on my bell but unfortunately I didn't want to allow him in anymore. My finger hovered over the red button momentarily before rejecting his call. I began to scroll down my contact list in search of a suitable distraction. My thumb continued to scroll until my eyes met with the name I had been searching for.

Junior Hamilton. My eyes lit up when his name illuminated on my screen. I was keen to see him for two reasons; firstly, because his deep dimple and his bright smile were to die for and secondly, I was sure that his performance and evening entertainment would lighten my mood. I squinted briefly as I contemplated whether I should call or text him but I was impatient. I wanted answers there and then so I slammed my finger on the call button. My fingers began to clam up as I waited for a connection. With every droning ring, my anticipation began climbing the walls. I leant forward eagerly awaiting an answer. The ringing continued then it stopped. Voicemail. My anticipation slumped as I flung myself backwards onto the bed. Saturated with water, the vision in my eyes became a blurry mess, yet no tears fell. I was in desperate need of a distraction. For a moment, I considered returning Nelson's call then my phone started to ring. My vision cleared and a small smile crept up on my face when I realised who it was. I inhaled deeply before I slid my thumb across the green button to answer.

"Good evening, Junior." I smirked in a low, seductive voice. My chest was warm but I played it cool.
"I never thought that I would hear from you," he began to confess. And I couldn't help but nod slightly; the ends of my lips pressed firmly down on my face. I was shocked, yet impressed.

“Really? You’ve changed your tune. I thought that you were pretty sure that you would be seeing me later?” I softly bit my lip in an attempt to hide my cheeky smile.

“Yes but when you took so long to call, I thought that you weren’t interested. Besides, a pretty girl like you probably has a load of guys chasing after you so I could be one of many." I listened suspiciously. Whilst he was very flattening, I was unsure how genuine his compliments were.

“Well, a girl must keep her options open as you never know what opportunity may come knocking on your door." I giggled internally.

“Does that mean that you will take the opportunity to come out with me this evening and see me perform?” For a split second, my whole face shifted upwards. I knew that was the invitation that I longed to hear.

“I don’t see why not. When are you coming to get me?” I brashly replied. I enjoyed wearing the trousers and they fit me well.

“I can meet you at the front of your hotel at 10 and I will call when I am 5 minutes away," he responded efficiently. Very organised indeed.

“Sure. That sounds like a plan. I’m going to start getting ready soon so I will speak to you later," I said as I steered the conversation to an end. Time was pressing and I had to look dazzling.

“Alright. Talk soon," he ended. Eager to freshen up and make a lasting impression, I began to strip off my clothes and stepped into the shower.

~ Chapter 7 ~

I stood patiently outside the hotel gates as I awaited Junior's arrival. Though the sky was painted black, a humid heat lingered in the air. The sounds of croaking crickets haunted my ears as I held my spot, alone on the street corner like a call girl. I was almost sure that someone was going to drive up to me and ask me how much I charge. Blindness filled the street as I stared into the distance with the only source of light coming from the cabin that they called the security office. It was more of box than an office so it didn't do the street much justice. I began to search in my purse for my phone when two beams of light started to travel down the road. They were shining so brightly that they blinded my vision momentarily. The vibration from the vehicle intensified as it neared towards me. The vehicle slowed, then stopped right in front of me. The music halted. I could hear the pounding of my heart in my eardrums as the window lowered. I only hoped it was who I was expecting. Then the tinted window revealed who was behind it.

It was Junior. My eyes gleamed at the sight of his gap-toothed smile and the heart pounding slowed. His smile was contagious.

A blast of cool air embraced me as I stepped into his freshly-cleaned vehicle. I was thankful for the air conditioning as the humidity was causing my afro puff to shrink. When I looked back, I noticed that there were 5 other seats, unoccupied in his car.

"Family man?" I eagerly questioned, desperate to find out if he was also married with children.

"No. I'm an only child but I have a lot of friends that travel with me from time to time so the extra seats are needed," he openly responded but he didn't quite give me the confirmation that I needed.

"So, do your children enjoy the extra space in the back then?" I had no option but to cut to the chase and get wholesome answers.

"No. I don't have any children. I'm single and ready to mingle; that's why you caught my eye," he shared as he glanced over to me, briefly taking his eyes away from the road. I glimpsed back at him, silently impressed. It wasn't every day that I had the pleasure of meeting someone who was nearing their thirties, still single and had no children. With his single, childless status confirmed, I eased back into my seat and began to enjoy the ride.

It was not long before we pulled up outside a club by the pier. Crowds of people queued outside the venue as they waited for the doorman to permit their entrance. Groups chattered loudly creating a show of themselves in a bid to be noticed; it seemed to be working. My eyes followed the groups of people closely as I waited for Junior to ready himself. But it wasn't long before Junior opened my door and waited for me to step out so that we could walk to the venue together. A few people stared at us as he led us straight to the front of the queue, which made me feel rather awkward but Junior seemed unbothered by the extra attention that we were getting. When we got to the front of the queue, the bouncer seemed very familiar with him and pleasantly welcomed us into the venue. Although I only smiled internally, I was extremely impressed by the V.I.P. treatment that we were receiving. It was something that I definitely could adjust to.

Junior led us to the V.I.P section where we were welcomed with bottles of champagne in iced buckets, an oversized bottle of dark rum and a few pitchers of juice. It seemed a bit extravagant considering we were the only two people there at that time, but I didn't mind. I began helping myself to a tall glass of rum and apple juice in order to relax my stiffness. Junior poured himself a glass of water, which was understandable as he would be taking the stage at some point in the evening. I was also aware that he was my designated driver, so I did not want to encourage him to get wasted. When we sat in our booth, we obtained the most perfect, private view of the stage and the people below. The leather seats were quilted with diamonds and my bottom felt snug as I sunk into the chair. A few people began dancing carelessly with their friends as they soaked in the rhythmic vibes. Junior didn't speak much but I could tell that he was pleased to have a woman on his arm. When the music halted, the crowds gathered by the front of the stage, knowing the show was about to commence. Casually, Junior placed his arm around my shoulder as the lights dimmed and the warm up act stepped onto the stage.

My head carelessly swayed to the music as the dancers performed. I was in awe of them as the dancers flung their hands and feet in the air, to the rhythm of the music. I leant forward in my seat for a better view as they swayed their shoulders down towards to the stage floor. It was impressive to watch how they worked their way up from the floor to fully standing again. The crowd jeered as one of the dancers back flipped and landed with their legs in a full split. The other dancers began parading around her as she continued to bounced her pussy up and down whilst her legs were still separated. Eyes wide, I turned to Junior both astounded and shocked but he looked back at me breezily. I could tell that he had seen those moves before. But as I looked back, another dancer began to straddle her shoulders as she continued in her split position. Then she leant backwards to place her hands on the floor and flip up and off of her. My head jolted backwards in amazement. It was a type of acrobatics that I had never witness before.

Just as I was starting to get comfortable, Junior mentioned to me that it was his time to perform. I held my breath momentarily at the thought of being alone in the booth. He reassured me with a light squeeze then disappeared down the stairs. I began pouring myself another helping of dark rum and apple juice, filling my cup with more rum than before. My lips pursed as I began to sip the drink slowly. The drink was sharp but it warmed my insides and eased my mood. Moments later, I saw Junior bless the stage and my heart skipped a beat. Guitar in hand, he began to strum tenderly as he sat down and rested his feet on the stool. I gazed at him intensely as his soulful voice echoed through the pier. The crowd swayed passionately with every lyric that he vocalised. They sung along in chorus as he belted out a tune that they all seemed familiar with. I had never heard the song a day in my life but it seemed to be a popular choice. I was amazed at how well the crowd responded to him and the vast size of his fan base. He began to finger the most transfixing acoustics on his guitar. Every strum felt as though he was plucking on my heart strings. Then he glanced towards me whilst on stage and my vagina began to flutter. Although I knew the beauty of serenading, I had never experienced it first-hand. His gaze was so intense that it penetrated my soul. My heart swooned as he sung to me and for that moment, it felt like I was the only one in the room.

When his performance ended, I rose to give him a standing ovation, truly impressed by his talents. I didn't expect his expertise to be that flawless. As he arrived back to the V.I.P area, I couldn't help but fling my arms around him in delight and he in turn, squeezed me tightly, cupping my waist.

"Wow!" I exclaimed in delight, grinning from ear to ear. I stopped for a brief moment to stare at him. His performance was out of this world and I was proud to be the woman on his arm that night. But before I could express my amazement, his distracted eyes searched the venue desperately.

"We have to leave now," Junior urged as he grabbed hold of my hand. "I can't stand the haste of people bothering me after a performance," he ended. Like a rollercoaster ride on full speed, a surge of excitement rushed through my veins as he lured me towards the stairs. His lifestyle gave me a rush that I had never experienced before.

"You were amazing on stage," I blurted out as he ushered me into his seven-seater. My heart was still thumping heavily from our race down the stairs.

"Thanks. Your beauty inspired me," he spoke softly as he strapped himself in. I stared back at him, gob smacked. *How could I have possibly inspired that show-stopping performance?* I knew the credit was down to his faultless vocals. "Let me get you home before it gets too late. I don't want any of your friends worrying about you." He commenced with turning the engine on. *Friends?* Eyes wide, I shrunk internally. Blood blushed in my cheeks as I remembered that I hadn't been completely honest with him.

"I'm on holiday alone," I uttered, unsure of how he would respond. But his eyes brightened as he peered over to me.

"Well, then I suppose I'll have to take care of you…" he gleamed. I giggled awkwardly, sceptical of how to appropriately respond to his comment.

* * *

The drive was silent and seemed longer than before. As I stared out of the window, the streets were engulfed with blackness and nothing looked familiar. As we travelled down the road, he slowed over the humps. My heart paused. It was at that moment that I had regretted telling him that I was alone. Paranoid thoughts of him kidnapping me and chopping me into a thousand pieces travelled through my mind. The car rocked from side to side down the winding road. I held my body stiff as the car wobbled. I had convinced myself that his decline in speed was so that he could park up and drag me out into the bushes. My thinking rate doubled. Automatically, I began conjuring up an escape route in case of an emergency. As I scanned the darkness, I only longed to see a familiar face or a familiar building to ease my nerves.

Before long, a light appeared in the distance and the street began to look more recognizable. The security box was in sight and I knew that we were approaching *The Vacation Lodge*. My thought rate began to slow and my fears subsided as he parked up just past my hotel. I hated it when my paranoia got the best of me.

"Thank you for tonight," I politely voiced. I was more thankful that I had been returned safely than I was for watching the show.

"No. Thank you. I meant it when I said that you were my inspiration." I glowed internally as he gazed at me with a lustful look in his eyes. I couldn't help but lower my own eyes as the guilt from my negative thoughts scolded me. I wondered whether my distrust for Nelson had caused me to doubt Junior. Junior had shown nothing but kindness towards me and I felt so ashamed that I had suspected his actions. My thoughts travelled back to the moment I met Junior at the beach. *Honesty is my policy.* The words rung in my ears. I shook my head in disappointment as I looked down towards my wretched fingernails. Calmly, he unstrapped his seatbelt and reached over to lift my chin with the cup of his finger.

"Let me see those pretty eyes of yours, Raven." He smiled, revealing his adorable gap. His dimple deepened as I looked up towards him. Our eyes met temporarily. My guilt urged my lips towards his; his eyelids began to close as my lips pressed against him.

Sparks swept from his lips to mine as they fiercely intertwined. Somehow, kissing him made me feel less guilty about doubting him and his intense touch made it easy to forget. From the moment his lips met with mine, I could tell that he was triggered as his fingers grazed deeply into my scalp. His firm hold made me feel wanted; it made me feel special. And as we advanced, I couldn't help but smooth my fingers over his warm chest as our tongues rubbed against each other like lapping dogs. As our

French passion grew more intense, I felt his hand slide up my waist and towards the side of my breast. My body gravitated towards his as I craved for him grab hold of my bosoms. His lips travelled down my neck and towards my earlobe, then he started suck on it like a hard boiled sweet. Like shutting blinds, my eyelids fused slowly as my lungs inhaled the deepest of breaths. The heat from his breath warmed up my earlobe and melted my heart.

Confidently, his hand began to glide upwards, brushing past the side of my breast as he reached for the zip at the front of my dress. Zealously, I bit my lower lip in anticipation of his next move. As his surging mouth worked his way towards the crease in my breasts, my fingers began stroking the back of his neck; slipping neatly in between his dangling dreadlocks. I exhaled deeply. He unzipped me. And my eyes couldn't help but roll back underneath my closed eyelids as he began to stroke his tongue around the circumference of my breast. *My, oh, my...* It was teasing at its finest. The more his tongue ventured, the more I encouraged him to explore. My vagina lips squeezed intensely as I rhythmically rose my chest towards his lips, urging him to go further. Though he didn't need the encouragement.

Braless, he eased his hot kisses towards my nipples as he cupped my breast tenaciously. I began to ride my hands up and down his head as I nuzzled his face into my chest. He flicked his fingers across one nipple as he rippled his tongue across the other.

Electric signals shot straight from my nipple tips toward my vagina, causing my pulsating pussy to intensify even further. My lips began to moisten; all four of them. As he continued tasting my torso, his penis began to swell; thick and sturdy.

Whilst he worked his way back up to the nape of my neck, he reached for my hand. He began guiding it towards his penis. My senses alerted. Although, I had allowed him to start discovering my body, I wasn't ready to feel his golden treasures. As he continued to drive my hand downwards, I resisted. But he continued and I froze. *Why wasn't he getting the message?* My hand repelled against his force even harder. Mid-resistance, he rose his head. His piercing eyes penetrated through me, as if I were nothing but an enemy of progress; an obstacle. My heart palpitated as he stared right through me. My chest began to tighten. His expression was blank but he continued staring into me as he drove my hand downwards.

Ba boom.

Ba boom.

Ba boom.

I could feel my heart throbbing across my chest. At that moment, I mentally prepared myself for sexual violation. And I regretted not listening to my initial instincts. I wanted to be anywhere but there with him.

"I want you so badly right now... touch it…" He whispered as he neared his lips towards my ears. I gulped suddenly.

"I don't want to," I bravely stated, hoping that he would respect my decision. His eyes shot to me.

"Why?" he questioned me as he eased his pressure. He backed away from me but my body remained stiff, numb from the resistance. I couldn't quite understand why he didn't read any of my signals.

"I just don't want to," I said as I mustered up the energy to zip my dress back up to the top. His force was petrifying and quite frankly a turn off.

"I thought that we were enjoying ourselves though?" He continued to probe me. From the look in his eyes I could tell two things; he didn't understand how to take no for an answer and he wasn't used to girls turning him down. This had put my back up.

"I was until you started to force my hand onto your cock!" I sharply responded. Any doors that had begun to open up to him were closing and were going to be locked shut. He sat back, checking his behaviour.

"Sorry, I must have been caught in the moment and started to get carried away. The last thing I would want to do is drive you away from me." Head bowed down, he glared up to me with a lost look in his eyes. A look that I had grown familiar with and seemed less effective the third time round. My eyebrow raised slightly towards him.

"Let's just leave it there. I'm exhausted and I have a lot to think about." My tone flattened. Although I felt slightly fearful and sceptical inside, I gave him a polite smile as I did not want to leave our conversation with a completely negative ending. "We'll speak," I finished as I backed my way out of his car, clutching my purse to my chest.

"I hope so. I'm sorry Raven," he whimpered as his solidness had subsided. Like a shrinking violet, The Incredible Hulk had regressed back into Dr. Bruce Banner. As he reverted, I could see that his confidence had degenerated, leaving him in an awkward mess. I read him for a moment before bidding him adieu; sadly disappointed.

I took a slow stroll back to my room. My feet were finished. I had a tremendous amount to process and I was overwhelmed by the thought of it. Junior was extremely generous towards me but I didn't know whether I was able to manage both versions of his split personality. Nelson's deception had disappointed me so much that I didn't know whether I could bear to speak to him again. *Why were they were trying to take advantage of me?* I couldn't get my head around it. I was stumped.

~ Chapter 8 ~

After an unusually long lie-in, my stomach began to grumble. Although the sun glared through my windows, I refused to rise early because my night's sleep had not been completely peaceful. Thoughts of my experience with Junior still haunted me, making it hard for my mind to switch off. Eyes tightly shut, I kept the pillow cupped underneath my head as I rested on my side. I left one leg cocked outside of the sheets which I used to cool me down because I was too lazy to turn the air conditioning on. Nonetheless, the heat from the sun persisted on warming me up. My thumb sat comfortably in my mouth as I attempted to ignore thoughts of the night before that were drifting in and out of my psyche. Even though I was nearing my thirties, I had always held a strong belief that sucking my thumb would help all of my problems melt away. And whilst not usually helping my problems, it always helped me to forget them. However, my stomach began to growl even louder and my thumb was no longer enough to fill my void.

I reached towards the bedside table in search of the food menu. I had become so entwined with my bed that there was no way that I was going to make it to the food hall that morning. Besides, it was nearing the end of the hotel breakfast times and breakfast in bed sounded a lot more appealing to me. I sat upright to scan the menu in detail. I was in search of something appetizing. And my stomach couldn't help but flip when my eyes met with my Jamaican dream. Salt-fish coconut rundown with boiled banana, sweet potato, cassava and fried plantain. My mouth began to water at the thought of it. Without a question, I lurched for the phone to order my breakfast.

As I waited, I flicked through the stations on the television for some late morning entertainment. I stumbled across a comedy show on one of the channels. The acting was so poor that it was actually laughable. Whilst I watched, I chuckled at the audacity that the producers had to air such nonsense on national television.

There was a stiff knock on the door. I leapt up in excitement as my stomach was somersaulting with hunger. As I opened the door, a plate of beauty blessed my eyes and my breakfast looked just as I imagined it. A whole, skinless, boiled banana smiled on my plate with a medley of sautéed bell peppers, onions and salt-fish doused in coconut milk. A few pieces of sweet, golden fried plantain complemented the company of the boiled cassava and sweet potato. I held the tray carefully as I carried it over to my bed. I ogled it once more before devouring the whole plate. Each bite was so smooth and the savoury enriched the flavour of the sweet as it kissed the back of my taste buds. By the time I had finished the meal, I was completely stuffed. Although I didn't want the taste to end, I felt as though I couldn't handle another bite of food for entire the day. My eyes began to grow heavy as my body endeavoured to process the food. I slid back underneath my covers to listen to the rest of the comedy with my eyes closed.

Knock.

Knock.

Knock.

There was a knock on the door, then a pause. Another knock forced my eyelids apart. I was shocked yet impressed at the efficiency of the bell boys in the hotel. Although it took me a while to process what was happening, I began to grab my tray and tidy up all of my wrappers. Then, there was yet another knock at the door, fiercer than the last.

"Room service." A voice from behind the door bellowed.

"I'm coming," I yelled back as I headed for the door. I could tell that the bell boy was growing more impatient by the tone of his voice.

Before I opened the door, I pulled my white robe over my bosoms to cover my modesty.

"Hello. Thank you," I politely blurted as I attempted to hand the smartly dressed man my tray.
His teeth clasped awkwardly through his smile then he giggled briefly. It was almost as though he was taken aback by something that he saw. I quickly looked down at my robe to ensure that I was completely covered.
"Thank you ma'am but these are for you," he politely responded as he revealed the most bountiful bouquet of flowers along with a golden box of chocolates. My jaw fell to the floor. I stood in awe for a moment as I processed the situation.
"Aaahh… Thank you." I squinted in confusion as I put down the tray to accept my delivery.

As I shut the door behind me, my eyes continued to flit between the flowers and the chocolates in awe of them both. A dozen pink, red and white roses encased in carefully wrapped tissue paper stood before me. A small, pink card neatly tucked into the bouquet. It was camouflaged so well that I barely noticed it. When I pulled out the card, it had only three words on it, *"Please forgive me."* My brain started to tick as I endeavoured to decode the message. I glanced over to the chocolates in search of more. The tray of chocolates were parcelled in a golden box with a brown bow. It had four small windows which revealed some of the chocolates inside the box. Behind the bow, hid a small card which read "Sweets for my sweet girl. Chocolates from your chocolate man." My cheeks flushed hot as I chuckled at the note. I had two beautiful notes but no name on either of them. I pondered as I walked over to the vanity table to place them down. I pulled out the stool that was neatly tucked underneath to take a seat by the table. I ogled the gift once more. I was desperate to discover who the gift came from.

Please forgive me… the phrase lingered in my thoughts. I examined the room in search for my phone. When I found it, I headed to the vanity table to take a photo of my gift. I needed to know who'd sent it to me. There were only two people that had let me down on this island and I was sure that it had to be one of them. However, I was determined to ensure that they both thought that they were the only person receiving the picture. I made sure to take the cards out of the image to increase the sender's anonymity and I scanned my contact list for both Junior Hamilton and Nelson Tannerman. I sent them both the image. My palms started to sweat on my phone as I awaited a response. Keen for a distraction, I began scrolling through my phone looking through all the pictures I had taken since arriving in Jamaica. A modest smirk appeared on my face as I glimpsed at the images of my first jellied coconut and the green guineps. As I continued to look through my pictures, my phone began to vibrate in my hand.

"Those are pretty," the message read. It was Nelson. I glanced at his message for a while as I tried to decipher his bland reply and whether his message actually deserved a response from me.
As I locked my phone, it began to vibrate again.

"I've been thinking of you," Junior replied. *"Did you sleep well?"* My eyes gleamed in pride. I was slightly impressed that he had shown such an interest in me.

"I slept okay but the sun woke me up early," I replied. I could see that he had read my message but I was interested to see how he would respond.

"Did you receive my card as well? My sweet girl…" As I read the message, blood raced into my lungs. My eyes widened as I read over his message again in shock. *My sweet girl…* Nelson wrote. I sought to the small card that came with the chocolates. *Sweets for my sweet girl.* And it clicked. Nelson had sent me the gift. My lips pursed in surprise that he had gone out of his way to apologise to me. My blinking multiplied as I sought for an appropriate response.

"Yes, I did thanks," I responded in brief. Not only was I in shock but I was unsure whether I wanted to open a conversation with him.

"I am truly sorry. I never meant to offend or disrespect you," Nelson typed. My eyes narrowed as I analysed his message. Although I was unsure how genuine his words were, the ice on my heart began to thaw as I read on.

"You seem like a decent woman and I respect you and your decisions." He began to type more, then stopped. I gawped at the phone, interested to see what he was going to type. I waited for a while but he didn't finish, so I responded.

"I appreciate that and I am glad you were honest with me." It was very noble of him to apologise and I respected him for that. It was rare to meet a man that admitted his wrong doings.
Moments after, he sent me an image with the caption *"Is this yours?"* It was a picture of my red, knitted shawl, diamantes and tassels inclusive. My eyebrows raced to my hairline.
"Yes!?" I replied. I couldn't believe that he had my shawl.
"You left your scarf at the Sports Bar when you left. I still have it with me," Nelson finished typing. My cheeks began to warm and the ice began to thaw a little more. Although I had completely forgotten that I had left it on the chair, I was so glad that he had kept hold of it. That was my favourite and only shawl that I had brought with me.
"Thank you for holding on to it. Can you bring it to the Launderette this afternoon?" I responded as I knew I had a load of washing to do. Not only that, I didn't know where my shawl had been so I thought that it would be a good idea to wash it along with all of my other dirty laundry.
"Can I bring it to you at 5 as I would have finished my shift by then?" he wrote. I was in no rush to wash my clothes so I agreed to wait for him.

My mouth began to dehydrate at the thought of seeing Nelson again after our previous discussion. Although he was off limits, I found it almost impossible to prepare myself for how awkward I would feel when we were finally face to face again. I had slept with him, found out about his wife then practically dry humped someone else. I flushed hot at the thought of it. Then my thoughts went to Junior. I quickly searched my phone to see if he had responded to me. I knew that he had read my message but he still hadn't replied. I assumed that he was busy and would reply when he had a spare moment. I tried to predict whether Nelson would be as nervous as I was considering the fact that he was so blasé at the Sports Bar. Both guys had my mind running on overtime. It was a messy situation and I was determined to clean it up one way or another. I poured some rum into a coke bottle to conjure up a more intoxicating brew that would quench my thirst. Whilst it tasted slightly bitter, it was just what I needed to make my meet with Nelson a little more tolerable.

As I sipped my concoction, I rummaged through my suitcase and wardrobes for my dirty laundry. All order had been lost and my clothes were everywhere. Underwear nestled in skirts, dirty entangled with clean; it was complete turmoil. In fact, looking around the entire room gave me a headache. I usually kept everything in a specific order but somehow I had allowed everything to spiral out of control and end up all over the room. Bikinis rested on chair backs whilst thongs resided on floors. Even my wet towel hung off of the corner of my bedpost. I hunted for the largest bag I could find and started dumping all of my worn clothes inside it. Before I knew it, the bag was filled to the brim and weighed a ton. I had not realised how many items of clothing I had actually been through. With all of the mess contained, the room appeared a lot tidier and the tension in my forehead began to alleviate.

Relieved that my room and my brain had been de-cluttered, I decided to play some soulful music to ease my mood even further. Bluetooth connected, Jamaican vibes blazed out of my portable speaker and vibrated through my soul. Jamaican music always had the power to take hold of me and relax my mind. The rhythms led me to the mirror where I examined my hips and waistline as it figured eight in time to the music. I couldn't help but bend over and watch my backside rotate as the rhythmic vibrations progressed. A confident smile appeared on my face as I inspected my moves in the mirror. Sounds of joy vaporised as I became more and more gassed by the musical beats.

Continuing the buzz, I danced all the way to the bathroom to turn on the shower. A jet of water spritzed all over my face as I used the shower head for a microphone. My head continued to bob as I lathered my body with soap but my feet grounded me as the suds slipped down the drain. My skin rejoiced as I scrubbed off the dirty layer and rinsed it clean. It was the freshest that I had felt for a long time. I reached for a fresh towel and snugly wrapped it around me. Wet footprints followed me to the bedside as I sought for my coconut oil. I sunk my finger deep in and drew out a glug of oil to lubricate my skin. Before it had even touched my palms, it began to melt and dribble down my wrists. I promptly smoothed my hands all over my skin and it was absorbed into my pores almost immediately. I reached for the coconut oil tub a second time, massaging the oil deep into my skin at a much slower pace. A quiet vibration crept all over me.

As I lowered the volume of the music, I began to lay down and enjoy the vibration. The longer I laid there, the stronger the vibration grew and the heavier my eyelids became. Imagery of Nelson taking me to a landscape of stables cultivated in my mind. The largest stables imaginable. As he escorted me round, he kept a tight grip on my waist as he introduced me to all the people that we bumped into; even the people he wasn't familiar with himself. Rows of black horses greeted us as we walked by their cages but there was one chestnut horse that had caught my eye. This horse had a long flowing mane, hazel eyes and thick, sturdy legs. His chestnut fur sat tightly over his sculpted muscles and I was desperate to take a closer look. As we stepped inside, the stable grew even larger. Golden hay swept the floor and kissed the edges of the wooden barn. Nelson led me to the horse and then kissed me gently on the forehead. I shared a lingering smile with him before he stepped back to let me admire the horse.

Sleek tufts of hair ran through my fingers as I stroked the back of the stallion. The horse allowed me to rest my cheeks on his neck as I twirled his mane. The stallion was so calm and gentle with me. I began to softly brush the sides of the horse to relax the stallion further. As I continued to brush, I noticed that the horse's penis was growing larger and larger. My eyes widened in shock. His penis was as large as Nelson's forearm. I stood back and headed to the gate in search for an attendant. As I turned around, the horse mounted me, resting his hooves on the barn gate. I tried to scream for help but as I screamed, not a sound left my mouth. I could feel his penis nearing my arse hole. In the distance, I could see Nelson canoodling with a woman that he looked very familiar with. I tried to wave him down for his attention but he was captivated by this woman as she fingered his chest. The chestnut stallion forced his way inside of me and started thrusting me aggressively. Bolts of tears streamed out of my eyes as the horse continued to tear his way through me. Struggling for words, I waved in Nelson's direction frantically trying to get his attention but the flirting woman turned him away from me as she laughed and stroked his shoulder.

One final thrust from the horse jolted me out of my sleep and left me gasping for air. I was in absolute shock and disgust. I began blinking frantically in order to focus my blurry vision. My eyes caught sight of the clock above my television and I sprang out of my bed. I was running late. As it was nearing 5, I quickly slipped on a maxi dress and brushed my face with makeup. I hastily rushed around for a hair brush and some gel to slick my hair into a bun. I found nothing more agitating than being late so I lunged for my flip flops as they were easy to slip on. Before picking up my bags, I topped up my bottle of drink, grabbed my phone and dashed out of the door. Although the weight from the bag weighed me down, I was determined not to keep him waiting too long.

~ Chapter 9 ~

Trudging my bulky bag through the hallways, I headed for the launderette. Some of the guests by the lobby bar looked at me twice as I lumbered on with my coke bottle in one hand and my laundry bag in the other; it was multitasking at its finest. It felt quite strange walking through the lobby and seeing a load of people lounging around as I had been in my room all day. The lobby rumbled with laughter as I worked my way through and I only wished that someone would have offered to lift the weight off of my shoulders. No one did. Most of the people were either glued to their tablets, searching for a Wi-Fi connection or playing boisterous card games with their friends. My shoulder began to grow numb. Hardly being able to bear the weight of my bag, I paused as I reached the end of the lobby for some respite. Instantaneously, I dropped the bag to the floor and rolled my shoulder backwards and forwards. Slowly the blood began to circulate back into my arms. Once I had achieved full sensation, I put my coke bottle in my weak arm and picked up my laundry bag to place it on my other shoulder. I marched on with pace in order to successfully make it to the launderette in the shortest time possible.

When I arrived, I saw Nelson parked on the bench, patiently waiting for me. He sat alone, opposite the washing machines as the launderette was completely deserted. He dressed casually wearing a fitted, dark grey T-shirt and tracksuit bottoms to match. He had changed out of his work uniform and his trackwear fitted him well. I smiled awkwardly as I fumbled my way inside. His whole face brightened as his eyes caught mine and he immediately lurched out of his seat to help me with my bag. I'd only wished that I had seen him earlier so that he could have relieved my body from the stress it was under in the lobby.

"Thank you!" I mustered up the energy to exhale as a sigh of relief. I slumped myself on the bench in an attempt to recuperate.
"No problem!" He smiled as he effortlessly placed my bag on the bench. He took a seat beside me and began rubbing my back endearingly. Although I was slightly unsure whether it was appropriate for him to rub my back, I was too tired to care.
"Are you feeling better now?" he jived as he poked me in my side. I turned to roll my eyes at him. I was still slightly upset with him for what had happened in my nightmare of a nap. Although he wasn't in control of my dreams, a small part of me still blamed him. I tried to brush off the feeling of disappointment that I had started to feel.

"Yes I am actually!" I replied before taking several swigs from my coke bottle.

"So, how have you been? What have you been up to?" he double questioned me. My eyes widened as I wasn't prepared. I couldn't help but hold my breath slightly as I thought about how to appropriately answer his questions without the mention of Junior.

"I've been doing a lot of thinking and trying to keep myself busy to be honest." I skirted around the truth as I took another swig.

"I tried to call you. I've missed you." He glanced over to me and my heart warmed a little. I struggled to stay angry with Nelson as he was always so polite towards me.

"I know. I saw your calls but I had a lot to think about," I responded thoughtfully with the intentions of being sensitive towards his feelings.

"Thinking about us?" He dug deeper. Guiltily, my eyes slipped to the side. It was true, I had thought about us to some degree but I had also thought about Junior and the trouble he had also given me.

"Yeah…" I nodded slightly as my cheeks began to blush.

"And how you missed me too…" He grinned cheekily. I raised one eyebrow somewhat as I smiled back at him and thought carefully about my response. Although I did miss his company and his quirks, a part of me knew that it wasn't right to spend too much time with a married man. I wanted to be honest without discussing my morals with him time and time again.

"I missed your jokes," I simply stated.

"And my touch..." He bit his lip tenderly. My lady walls twinged. He looked so delicious when he bit his lip like that. I rolled my eyes at him playfully before heading to my laundry bag for a distraction. I reminded my mini-me that he was a taken man.

Fumbling over my laundry, I began haphazardly loading my clothes into the washing machine. My eyes were fixed on the dial as I tried to figure out how to put the machine on the correct setting. I wasn't sure whether it was the lack of logos or the thought of Nelson's touch that was confusing me more. I was able to put my soap powder in the washing machine but for some reason, the concept behind the Jamaican knob seemed foreign to me. As I began fiddling with the dials, I felt his firm rod press strongly onto the crease of my backside.

"You forgot this," he breathed into my ear as he dropped my shawl into the drum. Although most of my body played stiff, my vagina muscles couldn't help but blink wildly.

"Thank you," I exhaled, patiently waiting for him to remove his piece from behind me. He didn't. I stepped to the side as I took a long swig from my bottle.

"Are you okay?" He jeered at my swallowing skills. The closer he got to me, the thirstier I became.

"I'm fine!" I flustered breathlessly as I turned to the dials once more. I was keen to be distracted from my burning desires.

"Are you sure?" he probed as he gently placed his hand on the small of my waist.

"Yes I am fine!" I waved, knocking my bottle of coke over. I inhaled sharply as I watched the drink splatter all over Nelson's dark grey fitted top.

"I'm so sorry!" I exclaimed, grabbing hold of my mouth mid-speech. My clumsy nature had gotten the better of me again.

"It's okay. I'm soaked but it's okay!" He chuckled as he pulled his top from over his head and began rubbing himself dry with it. My eyes twinkled as his muscles flexed all over his torso. He wasn't the only one who was getting soaked.

"Sorry. I was just trying to concentrate on the dials and you were so close that it was distracting me," I blurted out.

"Oh, I didn't realise I was distracting you." He winked. "But you know I am familiar with these types of machines so I can easily help you. Do you mind?" he requested as he signalled for his top to be put inside the drum as well.

"No. Go for it. It was my fault. The least I could do is help you wash it." I flurried as I moved away from the machine so that he could place his top in. I watched him carefully as he chose the right setting and started the cycle. He made it seem as simple as a snow drop. Water dribbled in as the drum began to swirl.

"That wasn't so hard now was it?" he joshed as he attempted to put his hand on my waist once more.

"Please," I urged as I stopped his hand mid-motion.

"What's wrong?" he queried, retracting his hand.

"You're a married man. It's not right for me to get too close to you," I explained. He giggled sympathetically.

"You really don't understand do you? This is very normal and does not affect my relationship at all. I can see that you are a respectable woman but anything that happens between us will not cause any disrespect." I tried to concentrate as he spoke but his perky pectorals were rather distracting. I closed my eyes briefly in order to focus on his words.

"I know what you mean but…"

"But what?" he interrupted me mid-flow. "You are on holiday. You should be enjoying yourself and I promised you that I would take care of you. When you're with me, you have nothing to worry about," he concluded. I squinted as I tried to read his thoughts. Whilst he was right about the fact that I should be enjoying myself, I wasn't sure whether infidelities were the best way of pursuing that.

"It's different over here. You don't need to be so uptight about things. Trust me..." He reached towards my waist once more. His hand lingered.

"I don't want to do anything that will upset your wife," I shared with him openly as I began to nibble the skin on my lip.

"I respect my wife just as much I respect you and I wouldn't do anything that either of you didn't want me to." He neared my neckline. "Ignorance is bliss. You are beautiful and you deserve to have some fun," he whispered as he gently sewed rows of kisses along my neck. I began grow weak to his touch and the idea of surreptitious foolery.

"Are you sure?" I urged for him to convince me further.

"You can't deny the chemistry between us. You make my heart weak when I see you and I know I make yours weak too." He continued to rub his lips over my neck. "Tell me if I'm lying." He drew me closer. His kisses made me speechless. "You see…" his thoughts were confirmed. We both giggled naughtily and in unison. "Anytime you want me to stop, just let me know," he whispered as he began to stroke his fingers over the meat of my buttocks.

Brushing my fingers away from my lips with his head, Nelson began to passionately rub his tongue against mine as he grabbed hold of my bottom firmly. My head felt weak. I smoothed my hands over his rippling back in search of support. The more he stroked my behind, the higher he drew my dress as he slowly drove me towards the tumble dryer. My fanny flickered as our lip locking grew more and more intense. A glint of thrill beamed through my black hole like a shooting star as his hard cock made an impression on my thongs.

As my back hit the tumble dryers, he reached downwards to grab hold of my thighs and levered me up onto the top of the lid. My dress rose above my underwear as he straddled my legs apart. The top of dryer felt stone cold when my bottom came into contact with it, but it didn't take me long to warm up. Beginning at my knees, he started caressing my inner thighs with his tongue. I began to giggle awkwardly as his head neared my underwear. "What's up?" He lifted his head to look towards me.

"The door is open…" I mentioned as I gestured my hands towards the gap in the door.
"So…" he winked as he proceeded on tracing his tongue along my thong line.
"I just can't with the door open like that…" I breathed as grabbed hold of his head. "Please..." I begged as my eyes spun backwards. Whilst I longed for his touch, I longed for privacy more.
He paused. I exhaled. He started for the door and sealed it shut. Before heading back to me, he dragged one of the benches from the middle of the room and barricaded it in front of the door.
"Better now?" he toyed as he came back in my direction. I couldn't help but smile as I shook my head at his cheesy nature. He smiled back as he began rubbing his nose along my thighs then onto my knickers. He inhaled my aromas deeply as he kissed on top of my underwear. As he continued to kiss my briefs, his lips rubbed against my clitoris.
He kissed me tenderly between each word, "Just...let... me... know... if... you... want... me... to... stop…" he muttered. I was once again… speechless. My instrument swelled with every kiss and my dome began to moisten. He drew my drawers down to my feet and kissed me once more. My body called out his name. Without delay, I cupped his armpits to pull his chest closer to me. Heart pounding, I began to run my tongue all over his chest allowing my fingers to follow the trail. His body was like a fine piece of art and I was keen to explore it. He smirked at me from one side of his face as I drew his track bottoms down his thighs.

A giant piece of wood protruded through his tight fitting underwear. My mouth watered at his sizable piece. I rubbed my mouth all over his boxers, hungry for more. He took hold of my chin and lifted it up as he reached inside his underwear to reveal his gun. With both hands, he grabbed hold of my head and sucked my bottom lip lustfully before urging me backwards on the dryer.

As I laid flat, his fingers began travelling underneath my dress and towards the centre of my chest. My body rose along with his hands. Gun in hand, he started to circle the tip of his penis onto my clitoris as his other hand massaged the essence of my breast in a similar motion. As I laid there, my pelvis couldn't help but gyrate as I lusted for his piece to complete me. But he wouldn't enter me. He drew my nipple out of my bra and continued to circle his fingers over my areola. "Just let me know if you want me to stop..." He smirked as he continued to thrust his penis around my clitoris, adding more and more pressure each time. My vagina craved him badly and the last thing I wanted him to do was stop.

"Don't... stop... please…" I begged as my world began to rock back and forth. I tried to grab hold of Nelson but he massaged my breast with such force that it made my body weak to him.

"I don't want to do anything you don't want me to. I will respect your wishes." He fucked with my brain. Although my head thought otherwise, he knew my body wanted more and I was desperate for it.

"Just the tip… that's all..." I battled with my morals. Whilst my body screamed yes, a small part of me whispered no. That part of me was so quiet that I could barely hear it over the moans that I released as he rubbed his dick up and down between my tip and entrance.
"Are you sure?" He toyed with my emotions.
"Yes… just the tip," I repeated, somehow convincing myself that the tip didn't count as penetration.
"As you wish…" he continued as he circled the head of his penis into my dripping vagina. He showed great control and respect of my wishes. He had put me in the driver's seat but I yearned to drive all the way home.

"Come closer…" I urged as I reached for his firm behind. But the force from his massage kept my back on the machine.
"If that's what you want…" Nelson gleamed as he thrusted his entire length inside of me. My body gushed with euphoria on his first stroke. And as he continued, all of my cares and worries poured completely out of me. My little lady pulsated as he drove his way in and out of me and my body tingled in awe of his every move. He drove his penis up me so far that I could feel his armstrong in the pit of my stomach. He thrusted, paused then thrusted again. The suspense drove me wild.

After a short while, he withdrew his unyielding penis and began to kiss all over my stomach. I missed the feeling of fullness as his piece left me.

He angled me over until my breast rubbed against the machine. He stroked his tongue all over my back as he kissed and licked all the way to my round cheeks. But I longed to feel him inside of me once more.

"Fuck me!" I begged, face down on the dryer. I couldn't take the suspense any longer.

Not a moment later, Nelson thrusted his penis back inside of me and I felt whole again. Pleasure palpitated all over my body as his hips persisted on bouncing off of my cheeks. The harder his strokes got, the higher his penis reached up inside of me. Although I didn't want the moment to end, my head felt as though it was about to explode with joy. My inner flesh was overflowing and plump. His thrusts got harder and faster. I floated higher and higher until I bursted with pride and he shuddered all over me. He exhaled a moan of release. I laid there, chest down, face sideways, absorbing the pleasure of the moment. He stayed inside of me until his mini-man retreated. It was at that moment that I realised that this holiday could be the best of my life, if I wanted it to be.

"You're right, I do need to loosen up more," I said as I laid there with my head in the clouds.

"Exactly Raven. You are on vacation. Just enjoy yourself while you can," Nelson whispered as he kissed me gently on my back. And for once, I listened and let go.

~ Chapter 10 ~

From the moment that I left Nelson, I couldn't get him off of my mind, nor would he let me. It had not even been 24 hours since I had last seen him, but I yearned for my next dose of vitamin N. Not only did I enjoy his passionate sex, but I loved his personal characteristics. He worked hard, he was kind and always respected my wishes. He was a reliable companion in the land of the unknown and he always made the effort to make time for me. He was the perfect way to keep me occupied while I was abroad.

I slept well after my rendezvous with Nelson in the laundry room and I had been messaging him since I woke in the morning. I rolled around on top of my sheets as we fired messages back and forth between each other.

"I can't stop thinking about you," his message read. I began to blush in excitement as I felt the same. *"Neither can he,"* the caption read on the image that he sent me. It was a picture of his fully erect penis, bald head inclusive. I burst into laughter as I twiddled my

toes. It was clear that he was proud of his piece and I had no doubt in my head why. He was so large that he could fill a full-sized Pringle tub.

"Oh, really?" I toyed, *"How do you know?"* I knew that I had made an impression on him because our chemistry was undeniable but I was eager for him to confirm my beliefs.

"He can't stop talking about you," he wrote. *"About your smile, your laugh and how soft you feel inside."* My eyes wound back in my head as I finished reading. A one-sided smirk began to appear on my face.

"He told you all that, did he?" I replied. Although I knew he was stretching the truth, his corn made me smile.

"Yes. He was telling me about all of the things he wanted to do with you as well… but I don't think you want to hear about that." He flirted with my emotions.

"I'm open to suggestions…" I held my phone tight in my hand as I awaited his response.

"Well, just remember it was him that said it, not me," he teased.

"Go on…" I pressed with open ears and eyes.

"He asked me to ask you whether you liked playing games?" he probed.

"I do as a matter of fact." I entertained his charade, biting my lip in anticipation.

"Have you ever heard of hide and seek?" he asked.

"Yes…"

"Good, 'cos he can't wait to find what you have hidden in your playroom!" he fired back.

"Ha ha!" I giggled like a schoolgirl.

"He also said that he couldn't wait for you to bounce on his pogo stick." My cheeks began to gleam as I read on.

"And that he was dying to dip his footballs in the back of your net." My mouth gaped open at his brazen attempt to tell me his cheeky desires.

"Wow… Your penis has a lot to say for himself!" I bantered back.

"I know, sometimes I think he takes it too far, but what can I say? He has a mind of his own," he brashly replied.

"I bet he has!" I sassed.

"But seriously, I do want to see you again," Nelson advanced, slightly altering the tone of our conversation. As much as I enjoyed sending saucy messages, I was dying to see him again too.

"When?" I asked.

"Today!" he wrote promptly. I liked his style. Blunt and to the point.

"What did you have in mind?" I eagerly enquired.

"Ever been to Dunn's River?" My stomach flipped in excitement, eagerly anticipating his invite.

"No…"

"Let's go!" he commanded. My eyes gleamed. Climbing Dunn's River had been catching cobwebs on my bucket list and I had a burning desire to cross it off.

"What time?" I keenly responded.

"Noon. The River closes early and it's going to be a long drive." I read, slightly confused. *The river closes?* I thought it was a weird statement to make but I simply responded with a thumbs up.

"Don't forget to pack a change of clothes. It gets wet down there." My nostrils flared as I read his message. I wasn't sure whether he was trying to be cheeky or serious but I gave him the benefit of the doubt as I cut our conversation short. It was nearing noon and I wanted to look my best for our trip.

I darted to the bathroom in search of some hair removal cream. Bristles of stubble had started to appear underneath my armpits and they were bound to be on show during the day. I slabbed a layer underneath my arm and turned on the shower whilst I waited for my hairs to wilt. After the temperature of the shower had warmed up, I stepped in and began to scrape away my undesirable stubble. The more I scraped, the larger the feeling of contentedness grew inside of me. I smoothed over my arms as I watched the hairs tumble down the drain. They were baby smooth. I couldn't help but grin from ear to ear as I soaped up in the shower. The messages Nelson had sent me relayed in my head and it only strengthened my urge to see him again. Conscious of the time, I rinsed off quickly and rubbed myself dry.

After I had oiled up, I headed to my wardrobe in search of my olive-green monokini. It was brand new in the packet and I had been waiting for the perfect opportunity to wear it out. I loved the way it looked on me. The monokini wrapped round my shoulders and the centre of my back to support the shape of my breasts. Though the costume covered my collar bones, it was complete with cut out cleavage which made my bust look appetising. The material covered my stomach and private parts but the waistline in the costume had also been defined to accentuate an hourglass figure which I didn't naturally possess. I was shapely but not hourglass shapely. Strings travelled from the front of my hips to the back and were only joint by a modest piece of material that covered my crutch and my crack. I winked at myself with pride when I examined myself in the mirror. I looked spicy. I wore tight denim hot pants over my swimming costume and a black, floor- length, mesh cover up which covered nothing at all to be quite frank; it simply blurred my sexiness.

I began to search my hotel room for a fresh towel and spare change of clothes. I had two outfits; a skin-tone midi-dress and an all-black playsuit. I couldn't decide on which one to wear so I packed them both into a small black rucksack, along with some underwear, my tinted glasses and some money. I caught sight of my untamed bush in the mirror and automatically winced. The hair on my head was long, thick and wild. Whilst I loved my coily locks, I knew that if I left it out, it would surely shrink into a tiny ball of nothingness the moment that it laid eyes on the river water. Immediately, I reached for the comb and began plaiting two cornrows down either side of my head. I finished by plastering my hair with gel that would control my edges. It was a simple but effective style for ease and beauty.

Make up done and I was ready. I sought to the last message he had sent me to confirm where we were meeting. It was his day off and I knew that he probably wouldn't want to enter the building so I decided to head for the security gate. It was a bright day outside and there wasn't a cloud in sight so I didn't mind soaking up some vitamin D whilst I waited. As I walked through the lobby, it felt as though all eyes were on me. Almost everyone that I passed greeted me with a good afternoon and a genuine smile. I had no doubts why it seemed as though everyone was being extra hospitable. My mesh cover up was rather revealing and even I noticed quite a few members of hotel staff double taking as I walked by them. My chest rose with pride as I sauntered by; the looks had confirmed what I already thought.

From the moment I stepped outside, the sun beat down on me. It was a sweltering day and the breeze stood still. Immediately, I reached into my bag for my sunglasses and sought shade under a tree by the security box. The heat was slightly too much to handle. I watched the cars pull up and leave outside the hotel as I waited. Plenty of cars drove by collecting and dropping off passengers but I still couldn't see Nelson. A sense of unease started to fidget in my fingers so I pulled out my phone for comfort. I scrolled to his messages. *"5 minutes,"* he had written five minutes before but still, there was no Nelson. I started to type, *"Where are you?"* I loathed waiting on people.

"Round the corner. I soon come," he wrote back. I weren't sure what corner he was around because I was on the corner and I could see clear into the distance.
"How long will you be?" I asked
"About 5 minutes," he swiftly responded.
"You said that 5 minutes ago!" My lips began to purse at his tardiness.
"That was a Jamaican 5 minutes but I will be there in an English 5 now," he shot back. Although I was slightly annoyed, I decided to give him the benefit of the doubt.

Moments later, an all-white, compact car began to slow outside of the hotel. I noticed that the white was fading on parts of the bonnet as the car staggered to a halt right in front of me. I sized up the vehicle as the passenger window lowered.
"I wasn't that long now was I?" Nelson grinned at me and my expression automatically mirrored his. Blood pounded out of my heart as I met with his bright eyes again. "Jump in!" he insisted as I paused on the corner. With a stiff tug, I was able to pull the door open and get comfortable on the passenger's seat. I could tell that the car had been around the block and then some so I made sure that I added extra attention when handling the car parts. As soon as I got into the car, he reached over for a hug. I inhaled deeply as his hands lingered on my waistline.
"Hey…" I breathed as I relished our embrace.
"You good?" he confirmed as he loosened his grip from me. I nodded coyly. All of the fire that I had over the phone had fizzled

out of me and I was now just a glowing wick. "You look it." He winked as he attempted to flirt with me.
"Thanks." I blushed as I fumbled for the seat belt. I dragged it around me and tried to force it in the buckle but it wouldn't lock. Nelson had noticed the baffled look on my face.
"Oh, don't worry about that. I gave up on that seat belt a long time ago. Just sit back and enjoy the ride." He smiled at me as I began to giggle. Nelson forced the car into first gear and the engine roared as we zoomed off down the road. The car was louder than usual and I could hear all of the rumbles and jolts as he maneuvered the car through the bumpy lanes.
"Are you sure this car will make it to Dunn's River?" I toyed with him as we hobbled along.
"Don't worry, I have had this car a long time and it has not let me down once," he reassured me. Even though I wasn't worried in the slightest. Spending time with Nelson was teaching me how to ease up a little. Only a little though. But this time, I was more excited than anything.

I stared out of the window as we drove along the coastline. Goats roamed the streets, carelessly chewing the grass in their herds. The grass grew quite tall so food was plentiful for them. The nature looked wild. Stray cats and dogs traipsed along, hunting for food as we travelled through small towns. Every now and then we would pass barefooted vendors selling bottles of drink and crisps. They would sit on a small wooden chair and wait for passers-by to hold an interest in their stock. It was a very lazy way to sell but it seemed to work nonetheless. I had been tempted to ask Nelson to pull over to support the local vendors on more than one occasion but he seemed determined to get to Ocho Rios for the falls.

In the distance, I could see a whirling cloud of smoke and a strong whiff of burning rubber entered the car. For a moment, I feared that the car was about to fail us.

"What's that smell?" I questioned as I brought my concerns to Nelson's attention.

"Oh, that's just burning dog and garbage," he casually replied. My eyes widened in shock.

"Burning dog?" I reconfirmed in disbelief.

"Yes, if the dog is old and dying, people will burn their dogs with their garbage to kill two birds with one stone so they can get rid of it all," he educated me. I squinted at him for a while, still in shock. It was a surprise to hear that people did that but I suppose it was understandable; they had to get rid of their trash some way or another. I could see that Nelson had sensed my slight disgust.

"This is a third world country you know. We don't always do things the way you do," he jived.

We had been driving for over an hour and my stomach had begun to rumble. I had been rushing to get ready so much so that I had completely forgotten to make time for lunch. The longer we drove, the more my hunger panged. Not too far in the distance, I noticed a drive-thru highlighted with the sign *Island Grill.* My eyes lit up. I begged Nelson to pull up so that I could order some food to cure my crippling hunger. The menu looked appetising. There were quite a few options that caught my eye; stewed peas and rice; jerk chicken, festival with salad and Fish burger and fries. I chose the latter as I thought it would be the easiest to eat as we drove.

My stomach rejoiced as I took an enormous bite out of my burger. I had never tried a fish burger that had so much crunch and spice yet almost melted as I bit into it. I wasn't sure whether it tasted so good because it was unusual or because I was ravenous. Either way, I couldn't care less. The fries were skin-on and actually tasted like slithers of potato. It was my first taste of Jamaican takeaway and I was loving every part of it.

It was not long before I saw a sizable dark, wooden notice that read *Dunn's River falls and Park* ahead of us. The writing was thick and white so it was clear to read from afar.

"There it is!" I yelped like an excited child. Nelson gave me an endearing wink as he glanced in my direction. We slowed to pull into the car park and search for a space.

Pebbles crunched as we tread the ground in search of the front desk. Crowds of people headed in the same direction and we followed suit. I raced forward, eager to start our excursion, dragging Nelson behind me. Before long, we were faced with an enormous queue which seemed almost as long as the river. I was

astounded. Loads of tourists came to Ocho Rios specifically for this attraction and I had underestimated the popularity of the river.
"You see. That's why I said we need to be here early," Nelson mentioned, gesturing to the queue.

After taking a moment to analyse our surroundings, I noticed two different signs above the tills. One read *Visitors and Tourists* and the other read *Residents only*. When I looked at the queues, I could see a visible difference in the length of them. The resident queue was significantly shorter than the other. My eyes brightened.
"Can't we go in the 'Residents queue'?" I asked Nelson.
"But you are not a resident." He laughed as he shook his head.
"Yes, I know but you are…" There was nothing I couldn't stand more than waiting, especially in long queues. "Don't worry. If we queue there, I won't talk. No one will know the difference," I continued. Nelson began to smile at me.
"I like your style." He winked as he led us to the shorter queue. As we neared the front of the queue, I stood mute so that the staff couldn't suss me out. I allowed Nelson to do all of the talking and I took a back seat. Within moments, he had managed to get us two tickets to the river at the local rate. We had saved over 70% on the entry fee and I was impressed. Hanging with Nelson definitely had its perks.

As we walked down to the entrance of the river, assistants stood behind a rows of stalls selling various goods which were aimed at allegedly enhancing our river experience. Some sold water shoes whilst others sold swimming costumes and river themed towels. Selling goods seemed to be a common theme no matter where I travelled in this country. I laughed internally. It was clear that everyone was out to hustle day and night.

After we had placed our belongings in the lockers, we were led to a young, energetic man who referred to himself as Stooky. He was coffee brown in colour and had shoulder length dreads which bounced when spoke. Although he was quite thin in stature, he was athletic looking and his blue wetsuit accentuated the tone in his muscles. He wore both a nose and a tongue ring which matched the silver sparkle in his eyes. Stooky was a very animated man and his hands flew about as he introduced himself and the river to us all. He told us that he was going to be our leader for the day and that he would ensure that we had the best time of our lives. We were in a group of about 20 people and he made us all hold hands and chant random Jamaican sayings at the top of our voices whilst we walked to the bottom of the falls.

When we reached the bottom, I peered up at the falls. Avalanches of water tumbled down the sky scraping rocks and caves. Canopies of trees clouded the sunshine as they swayed over the blowing water. I could see groups of tourists holding hands as they attempted to tackle the steepness of the river. They were so high up that they looked like an army of zig-zagging ants scaling the falls. As I took my first step onto the jagged rocks, streams of ice-cold water pushed past my feet and I could feel the slime from the algae in between my toes. The sound of the rushing stream was so deafening that Nelson could barely hear as I called up to him. My heart began to pound and I squeezed onto Nelson's hand a little tighter.

"Don't worry! I've done this plenty times before!" he reassured me at the top of his voice as he escorted me up the slippery mountain. Stooky did a good job of keeping us amped up as we trudged up the waterfall; giving us rhythmic chants to repeat as he recorded our wild experience. Screams of laughter left our mouths in shock as he dashed freezing cold water onto our backs and encouraged us to splash the other people in our group. And I was almost sure that Stooky got cheap thrills from dunking us down the water slide in between the slippery rocks. He shared a cheeky cackle every time he hurtled one of us deep into the water.

When we finally reached the top, Nelson grabbed hold of my waist as he pulled me close.
"We made it!" he breathed as he stared down at me with his glistening eyes. My blinking slowed as I tiptoed to reach his lips. His hand cupped my bottom as he bit my lip tenderly and my heart began to smile.
"You make a beautiful couple!" Stooky smirked as he walked past us and up the final steps.
"I've been trying to tell her," Nelson cracked back as he shared a wink with me. My cheeks felt rosy. As he reached down towards

me, my cheeks began to glow even more vividly. He pressed his lips deeply into mine as he twirled his head slowly and more passionately this time. And for a moment, I actually believed that he was mine.

"I've been dying to do that all day." He smiled at me. My lip began to curl on one side of my face as I stared back at him, dazed. "Do you want to chill on the beach for a while?" he suggested as we took our final steps to the top of the falls.

"Sure, I don't mind. We might as well make a day of it!" I agreed as I peered up to him. Nelson took hold of my hand and we leapt down the copious amount of steps which led to the beach front.

~ Chapter 11~

The sea was engulfed with inflated floats and tourists roaming on kayaks. Ahead of me, I could see a few members from our excursion group tumbling around in the sea. I began to strip down to my monokini as I was keen to join them. As I stripped, I could feel Nelson's eyes ogling me as if he were undressing me with his eye balls. My inner goddess stood proud as I could tell that he wanted a piece of me. Though I played down my excitement, I relished in the feeling that someone was attracted to me just as much as I was attracted to them.

Not too far from us, I could hear a man hollering, "Sky juice! Sky juice!" as he pushed his battered wooden cart down the beach. Hollering seemed to be the norm on this island but it appeared to be a good way of getting the attention of passers-by. He waved colourful bag of ice in the air as he shouted, "Come and get your Sky juice!" A small crowd of locals gathered. I could see them purchasing the bags of the colourful, crushed ice and they began to suck the juice right out of the bag with a straw. I had never seen anything like it; a slush puppy in a bag. I loved having authentic experiences and this was one that I wasn't going to turn down. The vendor attended to my order in such a complementary fashion; with his well-mannered advances. He was a scrawny looking man yet he managed a hefty machete with poise as he chopped off flakes of ice from a big block. Then, he poured colourful liquids into the bag and handed it to me. Although I found it quite awkward to drink at first, I couldn't deny the delicious taste as a cure for my thirst.

Way past the shoreline, I noticed a huge, green and yellow trampoline immersed into in the middle of the sea. My cheeks and eyes glistened in unison.

"Can we go on the trampoline?" I begged like a giddy child.

"Sure. Why not?" He chuckled.

"I'll race you there!" I spurted as I dashed towards the sea. The wind pulled my cheeks backwards and lifted my plaits upwards as I ran as fast as my legs would carry me. When I looked behind, I saw Nelson's powerful thighs gaining on me with a determined look on his face. He was taking this race seriously and it awakened my competitive nature. The water splashed as my legs crashed into the sea and my hands fought against the current. My breaths began to quicken as I neared the trampoline.

Suddenly, I felt two strapping arms grab hold of my waist from behind and haul me backwards onto what felt like a thick and firm surprise.

"Never try to race a Jamaican!" he huffed as he pulled me closer. He kissed my cheek hungrily. The splashes of water on his face rubbed on to mine as he leaned his head on to me.
"There's no harm in trying…" I giggled breathlessly whilst I turned to face him. My eyes smiled as I stared into his and I automatically leaned in for a smooch. I gazed into his eyes momentarily and he pulled me in once more. Lifting my thighs and straddling them around him, I felt weightless in the water. I smiled internally as we bobbed along, kissing passionately in the sea. We barely even noticed the white noise of chatter and laughter that surrounded us. His lips felt velvet smooth and they were so plump and juicy to bite. My heart began to pound and naturally, I wanted more of him.

There was a loud twang as my head bumped onto one of the trampoline legs. The shock of the hit interrupted our moment and we both shared a chuckle. He gave me a look to ensure that I was okay and I reassured him with smile.
"Up or down?" he proposed and a cheeky look almost immediately formed on my face.
"Up then down…" I winked as I reached for the steps of the ladder. Strips of water dripped off of my legs as I clambered up the ladder and onto the trampoline bed. Nelson followed shortly after. The bed was so high up that we had an almost bird's eye view of the beach. The sun caressed my back as I lay flat on my stomach, taking in the all-encompassing view.
"It's amazing up here," I said as I gaped.

"I know and private…" he added as he spread his hands up my back and towards my shoulders. As I looked behind me, I noticed the growing smirk on his face that seemed to be contagious. A sweet groan left my mouth involuntarily as he continued to smooth his fingers all around my back in a twirling then firm motion. And my head was forced to rest on my hands.

"Mmmm… that feels good…" I whispered as my eyes began to close. Though it was hot, blood persisted on rushing to my follicles, making my hair stand on end.
"Hush baby..." He whispered back as his hands worked their way down my back and onto my thighs. My lady lips began to open as the force from his hands separated my thigh muscles apart. He held my thighs firmly as he circled the meat on them outwards. The more he circled, the more my head began to swirl. My vagina smiled as his hands maneuvered up my thighs and onto my bottom cheeks. He began to kiss them as he squeezed then released his hold of them. With every kiss, I could feel my fanny flutter with joy.

"Turn around," Nelson urged. "I have an even better view for you." He smirked.
As I sat up, I noticed his stiff cock almost bursting through his wet swim pants. It was clear that he was full of just as much anticipation as I was.

"Rest your head on me," he commanded as he pulled my shoulders backwards onto his crotch. My head rested next to his bulging penis and it smelt delicious.

I stared up at the almost cloudless sky. A few whimsical shapes floated by as I focused upwards but nothing significant enough to make a clear image or block out the sunlight. As he rubbed my shoulders, I was in awe of the sky's natural blue beauty. I felt so small yet so important to the vastness of the universe. It was at that moment that I understood that life was too short to be anything but happy and grateful.

My eyes began to shut down as his fingers ran across the circumference of my breast and brushed past my nipples. His torso began to block out the sunlight when he towered over me to reach his hands towards my stomach. I inhaled deeply. My back arched willingly as he persisted on rubbing his hands forwards and backwards from my stomach to my breast. And my nipples couldn't help but stand on end as he fondled his fingers over them. The more he reached forward, the lower his hands reached until his fingers traced the outline of my vagina. And as he retreated upwards, he gently pulled on my kitty lips, taking a piece of them with him. My eyes spiralled back as he teased me, now stroking a single finger in between my lips as he repeated on rubbing my entire torso up and down. Small waves of joy amplified through me each time his finger toyed with my little lady during my chest massage.

My legs spread wider as I invited his touch and his fingers lingered. They lingered on my vagina, only rubbing backwards and forwards on my pubic arch. I could feel his fingers massaging my clitoris as they stroked back and forth and my hips began to rise. My breaths deepened as he goaded my clitoris round and round and I yearned to feel his fingers inside of me. I licked my lips gently as I reached to kiss his thighs. The smell of his dick was sensational and I longed to taste it but he lifted my head as I reached towards his penis. He maneuvered my body until my legs were facing him and were spread across the trampoline. Blood raced to the tip of my clitoris as he began to circle it with his thick thumb alone on top of my swimming costume. His head lowered onto my stomach, kissing my pelvis tenderly. My senses were sky high.

"What if someone comes over?" I questioned, taking heed of the fact that it was the middle of the day.
"Don't worry. We'll hear the splashing. It's nothing," he reassured me as he placed his wet lips on mine. The sensation of his lips over my muffin was so pleasurable that I didn't need much convincing. As he continued to circle my cherry, my vagina began to sweat from the tender bites that he laid along my crotch line. The more he kissed and bit, the more he eased my lips out of the crotch of my monokini. My body welcomed the feel of his warm breath on my vagina. He then slipped my costume to the side to get a real feel of me and began to press his lips deeply into

my moist privacy as his thumb ran rings around my clitoris. As his mouth action grew more and more passionate, my head began to float. I could no longer tell whether it was tongue or his thumb on my clitoris but whatever he was doing, I didn't want him to stop. It felt so good.

"Mmm..." I moaned as he thrusted his finger inside of me. His sensual bites were driving me wild. With every slow thrust of his finger in and out of me, he planted a wet kiss on my clitoris. My hips danced with joy as I laid there; legs spread, without a care in the world. They began to move in time to his rhythm, making the pleasure feel a whole lot more intense. He began to pick up the pace. His slurps strengthened as he licked and thrusted his fingers inside me faster and faster and faster. His head dipped in and out of me faster than an apple bobbing contestant. Blood raced from my toes to my cheeks as my body was consumed in absolute pleasure. But as he persisted on sticking his fingers deeper inside of me, he ran out of steam and his clitoris kisses got gentler. Lustfully frustrated, I drove his head down, closer to me so that my vagina could feel more of his face. The deeper he fingered me, the more I rode his face like a jockey.

My g-spot swelled as he dug deeper, stroking it over and over again. I began to implode in ecstasy. My body could no longer handle the pleasure that was simultaneously being given to my kissed clitoris and my stroked g-spot. But he continued and my lady muscle pulsed and pulsed and pulsed. Sexy sensations raced all the way through me until my pulse erupted into an uncontrollable tremble. “MMMHHhhh...” I breathed intensely. The gush of heaven poured out of me until my body came to a still. Eyes closed. Smile wide. I felt as light as a feather.

Rosy-eyed, I leant forward to grab Nelson’s face towards mine and gave him the most passionate kiss I could manage to muster up. I collapsed on the trampoline bed.

“Stay with me," he requested in a compelling fashion. My head shot over to him in confusion.

“What?” I didn’t understand how it could be possible.

“Stay with me tonight in Runaway Bay. My friend has an apartment there and it’s not too far from here. I can’t bear to drive all the way back to *The Vacation Lodge* right now after our tiring trip and I’m dying to taste more of you.” He winked. My little lady pulsed once more. Although the offer sounded intriguing, I wasn’t sure how it was plausible.

“What will you tell your wife?” I questioned, keen to find out more about their situationship.

“Don’t worry about that. I’ll let her know that I went on an excursion and I’m staying with my friend in Runaway Bay. She knows him well," he replied nonchalantly. My motherly brow raised towards him causing him to smirk uncontrollably in my direction. He knew my answer was yes and I too couldn’t wait to taste more of him.

~ Chapter 12 ~

After our eventful day trip, we arrived in Runaway Bay just after 7pm. The apartment was situated in the centre of the town, close to the restaurants, bars and nightlife. We took an elevator to the second floor of the coral-orange building and walked down the long, parqueted corridor until we reached the apartment that we were staying in. The door handle was key coded and Nelson seemed to already know what code to key in to gain entry. His familiarity with the apartment made me slightly sceptical. Although I said nothing, I considered how many times he had been to this apartment and with how many people but I suppose that was none of my business.

When I walked into the apartment, I was fairly impressed. The floors were paved with cream marble and the walls were brilliant white. It was an open plan apartment with a single, rose-wooden island, differentiating the kitchen from the living room. The kitchen surfaces were white granite and they were so shiny that I could actually see my reflection in them. The rows of rose-wooden cupboards that encompassed the kitchen walls complimented the island and the maroon leather sofas in the living area. The apartment was spotless and it seemed more like a show home than an occupied flat.

Speckles of sand stuck to my skin, I tasted salty and felt sticky. Although I didn't want to declare it, I felt too dirty to be in the apartment and was dying to freshen up.

"Where is the bathroom?" I desperately asked.

"Through the door to your left of the kitchen," Nelson responded as he gestured around the corner. As I walked around, I noticed that there were two bedrooms. I couldn't help but wonder whether we would be sharing later on that night.

"Is your friend coming back tonight?" I asked inquisitively. Nelson's upper lip began to rise.

"No. He doesn't live here. He just rents out this apartment from time to time," he revealed.

"So... this is all ours?" My voice slowed but heightened in pitch. He nodded shrewdly. I sighed a silent sigh of relief. I was delighted at the fact that I had Nelson all to myself for an entire night.

The bathroom was bright and welcoming, complete with two fresh, white towels on the rack and a bar of soap beside the sink. My body rejoiced at the sight of the shower and I couldn't wait to hop in. Almost immediately, I stripped off and turned the shower on at full power. A mighty spritz of water burst out of the shower head and onto the walls. I couldn't wait to get soapy and freshen up. I automatically felt a lot more relaxed after I had a shower as my body was ready to unwind. I headed to the master bedroom and collapsed face forward onto the king sized bed. My body bounced up momentarily before comfortably settling into the memory foam mattress.

"You good?" Nelson sauntered into my moment of peace.
"Yes. Much better now." I smiled. "This is a nice place your friend has," I casually mentioned.
"I know. That's why I like to come down here from time to time when it isn't occupied." He walked over to join me on the bed.
"How does your wife feel about you going missing *from time to time*?" I questioned him with my eyes in mid-roll. I tried not to mention her but I just thought the whole situation was all a bit bizarre and still new to me. I didn't understand how any woman could loosen the reigns on her man to such an extent that it was okay for him to sleep at someone else's house.
"I don't go missing. My wife knows my whereabouts but she is secure enough not to be bothered if I stay at my friends place for a night or two." He brushed off my comment. I glared at him in suspicion. I queried whether his wife knew the full extent of what he was up to or whether she just really wasn't that bothered. I really didn't want to keep discussing her but sometimes my inquisitiveness got the better of me.
"So how many girls have you brought to this apartment. You seem to know the key code quite well," I goaded.

"Not many at all. I mainly come down here alone to get away from it all." He stared out the window but my eyes focused on his words.

"Away from your wife?" I dug deeper. I wanted know exactly what he wanted to get away from.

"Ha ha… Did you ever hear about what curiosity did to the cat?" He smirked. "Enough about her. What about you? What do you want to eat tonight? You must be starving!" he suggested. He was right. I hadn't eaten anything substantial since lunch time and my stomach was beginning to grumble.

"What's good to eat round here?" I asked.

"There's a bad-ass seafood restaurant that make the best Conch on the island. It's called *Pier Catch*." His eyes brightened as he spoke.

"What on earth is Conch?" It sounded like an extremely unusual creature.

"Probably the best type of seafood you'll ever taste. They say it's meant to be an aphrodisiac." His eyes pierced me playfully but I gave nothing away. "You want to try it?" he suggested.

"Sure, why not? You only live once!" I laughed.

"Well, get dressed and we can go!" he ordered light-heartedly.

"I think you'd better get in the shower too young man!" I fired back, gesturing towards his sticky fingers.

"Don't worry about me. Just worry about yourself young lady." His voice deepened and I began to giggle. Although I toyed with him, I loved it when he took command.

Without much of a choice in outfits, I decided to wear my skin-tone midi dress as it was easy to throw on. I untwined my plaits, leaving my coils with a more defined curl. My hair band neatly slicked the front of my hair back, leaving the rest of my curled afro out to play. I was a lioness with a mane and I was ready to prowl. Whilst I got my face ready, I could hear the water splashing as it hit against Nelson's body and the floor in the shower. He had left the bathroom door open. I couldn't help but peer over as he soaped up and got ready. Although the shower door was a distracting blur, his chocolate God-like silhouette was clear enough to see. Soap suds dripped off of his tight buttocks and muscular thighs. I ogled momentarily as his loaded biceps massaged his defined chest then his low fade on his head. *My, oh, my.* I questioned whether his open door policy was purposeful or just the way that he usually showered. Either way, I didn't mind as I enjoyed the moment.

After I had finished getting ready, I decided to get comfortable in the living area as I waited. My bottom sunk into the maroon sofas as I turned the television on for company. Although I would usually be frustrated whilst waiting for someone else, somehow I didn't mind this time. I felt at ease. Waiting on comfortable sofas felt a little different; more natural. It almost felt as though the place was ours and he was mine. I took pleasure in my fantasy and I didn't want anyone to burst my bubble.

Eventually, we were finally ready to leave and we headed for the stairs. My black flip flops flapped as I held onto his arms tightly and walked down the hallway. They weren't my usual evening attire but I didn't have much choice in Runaway bay. All of my shoes were at my hotel and I had only packed for an excursion. However, my flip flops were extremely comfortable to walk in and matched most outfits. It was only a short walk before we arrived at *Pier Catch* because we were so close to the town life. The town was filled with people leaving restaurants and heading to bars for drinks with friends. Local taxis beckoned to us as we walked down the road practically begging us to jump in their ride. But before we knew it, a bright blue sign flashed before our eyes. We had arrived at *Pier Catch.* It was practically empty so we walked straight in. As most of the chairs were unoccupied, we had the first choice in where we sat. Nelson decided to choose a booth on-looking the sea. We sat next to each other instead of opposite. From our seats, we could see a red, twilight glow stretching across the sea as the sun settled below the horizon and the tide crept in. The natural light reflected onto our skin through the window.

Nelson took the lead in ordering and we shared a three course meal. We had coconut fried shrimp followed by the infamous Conch in garlic and parsley sauce. My eyes widened as I saw the largest sea shell imaginable arrive at our table. The shell was twirled and pointed at one end. It reminded me of the sea shells that my mother used to collect when I was a child. My sister and

I would hold the sea shells up to our ears and listen carefully as we heard the seaside sounds flow through. When Nelson said Conch, I never expected that I would be eating this. It was a real taste of sea life and came served with fried plantain, a bed of salad, rice and red kidney beans. The food was plentiful and the Conch was surprisingly delicious. As we reminisced on the day that we'd shared, we wrapped ourselves up in laughter and chatted the night away. The time flew by and it felt as though the restaurant was ours alone as we spoon fed each other sorbet. I could tell that Nelson wasn't ready for our adventure to end.

"Why don't we go out for a night cap?" Nelson suggested. "There's a bar called *Enigma* not too far from here that I think you will enjoy." He smirked.
"Oh, really?" I smirked back.
"Yeah. Who knows when you'll be back in Runaway Bay, so you might as well enjoy it to the fullest," he persuaded me.
"That's true. I'll try anything once." I shrugged my shoulders nonchalantly.
"You would? Would you?" Nelson's lip began to purse suggestively.
"Well, MOST things…" I confirmed with a slightly concerned look on my face.
"Well, I reckon you'll enjoy *Enigma*," he continued as he signalled for the bill. "Let's go," he urged as he grabbed my thigh underneath the table. He bit his lip as he stared into me and my sex drive began to twinge. His touch had a powerful yet hypnotic

way of getting me to do whatever he wanted and I was fully aware of that. After leaving a generous tip for the waiter, he gave me his hand to aid me out of the booth.

~ Chapter 13 ~

We strolled hand in hand out of *Pier Catch* and onto the strip that was home to a stream of bars and restaurants. The streets were livelier than before and the music seemed a lot louder. As we walked on, it was not long before we reached the end of the strip. None of the bars were named *Enigma* so I was curious as to where we were headed.

Finally, we turned down a dim alleyway where the only source of light came from the moon. The pathway was quite narrow with dingy, grungy walls. I could see the paint peeling away from the surface in some patches as we ventured through. Down the alley, it was so quiet. The only sound that we could hear was the dripping drain as the water hit the pavement. Suddenly, two boisterous men wearing red bandanas around their face bulldozed their way through the alleyway barking aggressively towards each other. My heart pounded a little faster as they neared us and I held on to Nelson a little tighter. Sensing my fear, he wrapped a reassuring arm around my shoulder as they stormed passed us in a turbulent manner. The men seemed to be in some sort of disagreement and they were so involved with each other that they had barely noticed us in the tight passing pathway. To my relief, the men were no trouble to us as they continued past us and my pounding heart began to soften.

At the end of the dark backstreet was a jagged flight of stairs which led to a sizable car park. As we entered, vehicles vibrated with rhythmic sounds and began to fill up the car park. I gaped around in amazement. I was dumbfounded by the lively vibes that hid at the end of the eerie alleyway. Bubbly groups of people gathered in the car park whilst they waited for their friends. Street vendors marked the walkways with their smoking hot jerk pans. The car park led us to a green, illuminated sign above our heads reading *Enigma.*

A short queue formed outside but quickly disappeared into the bar. Before we knew it, we were at the front kiosk. Nelson slid some money through a glass hole to a lady who was sat behind it. I stayed close to Nelson as we walked through to receive our wristbands. When we reached the double doors. I noticed a sign which read "Respect the Rules: No Marinas, No Bandanas, No Bad-vibes, No Cameras". I stood baffled for a while as I processed the club rules. I had never been to a venue where picture taking wasn't allowed so I assumed it must have been normal protocol for the clubs in Jamaica.

When we walked through the big, black double doors it all became a lot clearer. On the right of us stood a bar, filled with bottles of spirits, wines and bartenders flapping around trying to serve us all as fast as possible.
"What are you having?" A meagre barmaid bellowed to me as she leaned over the bar. She was small in stature and wore a hair piece on top of her pony tail. I could tell that she was rushed off of her feet by the dregs of hair that fell out of her hair band.
"Can I have two rums with apple juice?" I requested recognising her struggle. I didn't want to fluster her anymore and I had no intention of queuing up for another drink any time soon. Nelson ordered his drinks with mine also to kill four birds with one stone. As she dashed off to make our drinks, I felt a warm hand impressed on my shoulder.

When I turned around, I was faced with a tall, slim and shaped woman wearing nothing but a corset. Her perky, brown nipples were eye-level with me and I couldn't help but gape at her. Her glass stiletto heels lengthened her limber legs and her lacy thongs accentuated the lift in her bottom. Her black corset was tightly fitted and cupped underneath her breasts; thinning her waistline and enlarging her hips. My heart plunged into my stomach. I searched for Nelson's facial expression to see if he was just as shocked as I was but when I looked at him, he only smirked.
"Do you want to dance?" she asked as she leaned over to reach my ears. I held my breath momentarily, speechless for a second or two. She looked as though she was East-African with her

toffee-coloured skin and her long, dark curls that twirled down her back. Although she was a stunning woman, I was at the bar with Nelson and not looking for any extra attention.

"No, thank you." I flushed hot, embarrassed for her nudity. I couldn't believe the audacity that she had to walk around half-dressed. But as I turned towards Nelson, I had noticed that there were quite a few women parading around topless and in heels. Trying to conceal my expression, only my eyes gouged open in shock. A few metres away, I saw what looked like a boxing ring. I noticed some of the topless women were walking towards it and some were dancing provocatively on the stage. I firmly pulled Nelson towards me.

"What sort of place is this?" I badgered him but his smirk only widened.

"Can't you tell?" He winked at me. Admittedly, I could tell but I almost couldn't believe it. Nelson had taken me to a strip club. The term strip club was used in the loosest sense of the form as the girls were practically naked already. No wonder we weren't allowed to take pictures inside the venue. I blurted out an awkward giggle in disbelief. I had never been to a place like it before but I was slightly impressed by some of the moves that the women were making.

A slightly rounded woman took stage in the ring. Immediately, she began spreading her legs baring her crotch-less underwear. As she balanced on her head, she began turning her waist and body in a 360-degree direction. Her hips slowly spun round and

round as she addressed all angles of the stage. Men and women began gathering on the stools that surrounded the elevated ring to give her tips.
"Do you want a closer view?" Nelson offered as he gestured towards the stage. I shook my head coyly.
"Let's go by the bar down there." I half avoided his question. He led us to a shadowy part of the bar which slightly hid our identification whilst still giving us a good view of the women on stage. We sat comfortably on two stools as we sipped our drinks. The girls danced and the guys gathered with their cash ready.

Moments later, my eyes were drawn to a miniature man with a dwarf-like stature who had just walked through the door. I was unsure whether he was so noticeable because of his hip-high size or the palpable confidence that he emitted as he waltzed through the room. Although his disproportionately, short limbs caused him to waddle when he walked, he still did it with style. He appeared quite popular as more than a handful of people went out of their way to greet him as he walked in and he humbly greeted them back. As the people endeavoured to welcome him, I couldn't help but wonder whether they were being so friendly because they knew him well or because of his disability. Despite that, it was noticeable that some of the topless women were keen to serve him.

After speaking to a few of the over-accommodating girls, one of them led him to the stage and he willingly followed. She was a fairly thick, pear-shaped woman, carrying most of her meat on her lower half. She wore her hair in a pony which was so tight that it drew her cheeks and eyes upwards. Though her breasts were small in comparison to the rest of her body, they were still quite large. They sat over her breast-less body suit that travelled through the middle of her chest and strapped round her neck like a dog collar. The lower part of the body suit was thong shaped, curving around her voluptuous behind. Her thick heels accentuated the tone in her calves as she strutted on.

Smooth rhythms boomed through the room as the meaty girl took centre stage with the pocket sized man. She began to move her body in time to the music whilst she slowly undressed him. Although his limbs were small, it was clear that he worked out as his chest and abdominals were clearly defined. She ran her hands over his pronounced biceps and down his stocky thighs. Her eyes gleamed as she got him down into his boxers and she began to lick her lips eagerly. Without hesitation, she drew down his boxers, revealing his thick, firm snake. My mouth hung open astounded at the size of his lengthy penis in comparison to his miniature body. He stood proud. The crowd jeered him on as he wound his hips causing his girthy snake to wave wildly.

The girl winked at the audience as she fell to her knees and wrapped her thick hand over his equally thick penis. Almost immediately, she smothered her lips over his piece and began suck him like a hoover on full blast. My head shot towards Nelson in disbelief.

"No! What?" I exclaimed as I grabbed hold of his thigh.

"Ha ha! Welcome to Jamaica!" he joked as he gestured towards the stage. Though I cringed internally, my eyes were drawn to the show. My eyes were fixed as she spun her head round and round as her mouth darted backwards and forwards on his penis. I'd never seen anything like it. After a while, he withdrew his still-firm snake and signalled for her to turn around. She turned around willingly, still on all fours and he pulled her thongs to one side. Her eyes spun back in her head and her mouth dilated, as he began to grind his way inside her slowly. He began to flex his muscles as he played up to the audience's cheers. I burst out in a laughter that was masked by the penetrating sounds of music that filled the room. I was in utter shock that two people were having sex in front of my eyes. Soon after, he stretched out his paw-like hands in an attempt to take control of her grand behind and daggered his way into her. Picking up the pace, he began to thrust faster, holding on to what he could manage. Her mouth widened in pleasure from the feel of his solid cock and the crowd roared. He then used her bottom as support to spin around so that his hands were on the floor and his feet were in the air whilst he was still inside of her. The people laughed in merriment as he bounced his hips off of her behind. It was clearer than ever why he had such a welcoming reception from the members and the club staff. He was definitely a showman with plenty of tricks up his sleeve.

As he finished off, the host welcomed another dwarf on the stage who favoured the first man. The crowd burst into applause after hearing that the two men were brothers. The audience sat up in their seats, eager to see the next instalment of a riveting show. Two ladies fought for the chance to please him as they lusted to feel the snake in his pants. Slightly coyer than his brother, he began to blush as the women undressed him and kiss all over his pint-sized chest. The crowd cheered him on as the women raced to remove his boxers. His boxers fell to the floor and the girls paused. Their eyes fixed on his pinky-sized penis. I grabbed my gaping mouth as I leant towards the ring to get a better view. I could see that his seed-like bollocks were even larger than his penis and the girls burst out in uncontrollable laughter. They continued their laughter as they tumbled off of the stage, leaving the midget man alone, stark naked in the middle. My face winced in embarrassment. His tiny paw gripped onto his handful whilst he scurried to collect his clothes from the floor. A small part of me almost died inside as I watched his tiny bottom waddle off into the darkness. *Enigma* was turning out to be the freakiest show that I had ever attended without a doubt, yet a weird part of me quietly enjoyed the entertainment. I sipped my juice giddily as I waited for the next act to grace the stage.

"Are you enjoying yourself?" Nelson boomed the question into my ears. The environment was so loud that we had to practically shout to hear each other.

"Surprisingly, yeah…" I smirked as my mouth lipped the straw to sip some more.
"I'm glad!" He smoothed his hand over my thigh causing my vagina to twinge pleasurably as I relished in his touch. His eyes smiled lustfully as he tried to read my thoughts.

The audience hollered, interrupting our moment, when the host welcomed a tall, caramel man to the stage. He was around 6 foot 4 with shoulders broad enough to carry the world. Already topless, he celebrated his athletic body as he flexed his six-pack. His muscles rippled as he ran his fingers down his stomach and over his crotch. As the music blazed, he danced his trousers down to the ground, followed by his briefs. A silent eyebrow raised towards him as I admired his full package. He was hung like a horse. A small part of me wanted to jump into the ring, almost forgetting who I came with. But moments later, a petite female floated onto the stage and started to circle round him in an erotic manner. She was sexy, slim and wore a breast-boosting bikini. And although her face wasn't that appealing, she commanded the stage like a goddess.

The gleam on his face widened as he stopped the female in her tracks and immediately started flourishing her in kisses. Slowly, he eased her bikini bra off as he slurped his tongue all over her neck. I watched in awe as her bikini top dropped to the floor. Picking her up, he grabbed hold of her bottom as he sucked her breasts hungrily. Her head tilted backwards as he plunged his head into her chest. My chest rose towards him as I imagined the sensations that she could feel. Then, he laid her on the stage floor and the crowd peaked forward like meerkats; watching his every move. I stepped off of my stool to get a closer look. I bit my lip gently as I watched him sweep his tongue all over her stomach and legs whilst pulling down her bikini bottoms. As his kisses lingered on her inner thighs, her legs spread willingly. I eased back onto Nelson rubbing my backside against his crotch. I could feel him getting firmer as I discreetly circled my bottom onto his piece. My eyes were fixed on the man on stage as he picked up the slim female, placing her legs over his broad shoulders. He lapped her kitty like a thirsty dog and my clitoris began to pulse. His head twirled round and round as he tasted her petite vagina. As I continued to watch, I continued rubbing my backside around Nelson's crotch slowly but more intensely. My breathing deepened as he ran his thumbs over my v-line.

Spinning her around mid-air, he lowered her on to his horse-like cock and penetrated her deeply. Her mouth groaned as he cupped her shoulders and buried his treasure inside of her. She began to moisten as he slid his way in and out of her and I could feel Nelson's hands creeping over my pelvis. His touch coupled with the view in front of me sent spasm of sparks through my soul. A deep throb started to emerge in between my legs and I longed for him to touch me more. During our moment, Nelson noticed that the East-African looking woman had been watching our every move and he signalled to her. She strutted right over.

~ Chapter 14 ~

"You want a dance?" she asked as she leaned her bosoms into Nelson. My venom-like eyes darted towards her. Although he wasn't officially, tonight he was mine and I didn't want to share.
"No, but she might…" he suggested as he eased her in my direction. My breathing halted almost immediately.
"You ready for a dance now?" She smiled in my direction but I was unsure how to respond.
"I don't know," I replied, making zero eye-contact with her. My lips dried quickly as I spoke to her. I had never had a lap dance before, let alone with another female.
"Don't worry, I don't bite…" she smirked, "unless you ask me to…" She laughed and I couldn't help but laugh along with her. Though I had never been approached in this way before, she did seem somewhat endearing.
"What's that you said about trying anything once?" Nelson whispered in my ear. "If you want a dance, I'll pay. It's all good." He stroked my shoulders. I thought for a moment, digesting his words. "You only live once…" he continued in my ears. I looked

over at her and somehow, having a dance with her didn't seem that bad.

"Listen, I can take you to a private room if you want?" she suggested as she stroked my hand.

"Only if he comes with me!" I giggled as I became more accustomed to the idea. I didn't know when I would have an opportunity like that again so I thought that I might as well do it for the amusement.

"Sure. No problem," she said as she took my hand and led me through the audience. I beckoned to Nelson to follow behind.

She took us to a much dimmer room with only just a few chairs. Although, the music from the main room blasted through the speaker in the side room, it had a much more intimate feel. She placed me on the chair and began wind her waist in front of me. Her bottom bounced as she twisted it round and round then she sat on my lap. It was perfectly rounded and I was almost jealous of her shape. Her slim waist snaked in and out as she slithered all over me. I glanced over at Nelson as she flipped over and began grinding her vagina on my lap. He smirked as he watched and I could tell he was enjoying it. The fact that he enjoyed watching us slightly turned me on and loosened me up. The toffee-skinned girl arched backwards, rising her breast and vagina into the air in a wave-like motion. The harder she grinded, the more her thongs slipped in between her lady lips. Surprisingly, the sight of winding vagina quickened my heart- rate and strengthened the impulse between my own legs. My mind raced in confusion. I was curious whether my arousal was due to her movements, the sights that I had witnessed on stage or the thought of Nelson enjoying what he was seeing. Either way, the throbbing in my underwear was hard to ignore as she placed my hands on her breast. I didn't know whether it was right for me to be enjoying it as much as I was. But as I watched her, I imagined me grinding on Nelson the way she was grinding on me and the thought drove me wild. I couldn't wait to have my wicked way with him.

Nelson reached for some cash and slipped it under her thong line.

"Thanks," she said as she stood up from on top of me.

"It was my pleasure," he added as he slipped his hand over my breast sending a spark to my sex. "Let's get out of here," he commanded as he ushered me to the door. I didn't need any convincing as I was desperate to have him all to myself.

We scrambled through the busy crowd and headed straight towards the exit. There were a few hefty looking men manning the doors but they eased to the side when they saw us urgently forwarding towards them. A group of smokers gathered by the stairs next to the doorway, lighting up and puffing clouds of smoke into the air.

"I want to fuck you so badly right now…" I whispered into Nelson's ear as the double doors shut behind us, muffling the intense blast of music in the venue.

His eyes lit up immediately. "Do you now?" he simpered, wrapping one arm around my waist then another.
"Yes!" I breathed as I pressed my hips firmly against his. I stretched onto my toes to give him the kiss I had been burning to give him all night.
"Right here? Right now?" he confirmed.
"Yes!" I urged as I took hold of his hand and lured him in the direction of the car park, which was now full.

I led us through in search of a private spot. Bushes rustled behind the cars and faint moans crept out of them. Clearly, I wasn't the only one who was feeling extra randy but I didn't care. I pulled him behind the final vehicle at the end of the car park and used my body to push him against it. I placed a sturdy hand on his equally sturdy cock. I immediately closed my eyes and bit my lower lip as I imagined what he would feel like inside of me. I inhaled his sweet aroma and unbuttoned his jeans.
"Go easy girl!" He smirked, lightening the intensity of the mood but I was too horny to give a fuck.
"Don't worry, I'm gonna take good care of you…" I shot back as I dropped to my knees and lowered his trousers. His briefs were looking extra tight as his bulge filled the breathing space in his underwear.
"You're looking a little claustrophobic down there… let me help you with that." I flirted as I pulled down his briefs. My eyes smiled at the sight of his thick, chocolate penis.

"Mmm..." I breathed after I inhaled the musky scent on his groins. "I've been dying to taste you all day," I finished before gripping the base of his penis and placing tongue-filled kisses all the way up his shaft. His snake was silky smooth and tasted delicious. I smiled internally as I felt him grow with each kiss. I could feel his meat caress my tongue as I sucked along the length of him, not yet tasting the tip. The more I tasted of him, the more I wanted. As I worked my way upwards, I finally wrapped my lips around his chocolate bell and inserted him deeply into my wet mouth. As I retreated, I laced my tongue on the back of his shaft before sucking his tip.

"Aaahh..." he exhaled and my cheeks began to beam with pride. I could tell that he was enjoying it. So I repeated sucking on the entire length of his penis like an ice-pole; and with every suck, I savoured the flavour before diving back in. The more he felt my warm mouth dip back down past his tip, the deeper his breathing got. I wrapped my hand around his dick and allowed it to follow down and up as my lips buried his penis deep into my mouth then retreated for air. I continued on swallowing him over and over again and every time I swallowed, his groans intensified. My vagina began to moisten at the sound of his enjoyment.

"I want to feel you inside of me." I craved as I stared up at him from down below.

"Come here." He grabbed me by the shoulders and pulled me up towards him. His lips locked with mine intensely and rushes of blood raced all over my body. He groped my meaty cheeks towards him, opening my hole and I longed for him to fill it. As he began sucking on the nape of my neck, he rose my dress upwards, revealing my plump butt cheeks. Eagerly, he grabbed me towards him and lifted my legs up until my feet were balancing on the side of the car. Automatically, I wrapped my arms around his neck for support. Bending his knees and leaning backwards, he began to thrust himself inside of me. The first thrust was the sweetest. I tasted my lips.

"Mmmhhh…" I couldn't help but moan in intense pleasure. My wet walls clenched around his penis. Noting the pleasure on my face, he delved his way deeper inside. As the sparks rushed towards my sexual organs, my head began to float. I could feel him caressing my sweet spot as he surged his way through me. My vagina began to moisten even more, allowing him to slip in and out of me faster and faster. I was swollen in pleasure. The more his meat kissed my sweet spot, the more I began to overflow. I could feel him pulsating inside of me and I knew he was close to climax. He started to thrust in me fiercely and my pleasure levels heightened.

"Don't you dare come before me!" I commanded. But I could tell by the weak look in his eyes that it was too late. Moments later, I felt his burst of ecstasy release inside of me as he clutched me tightly. My lip curled up as I gazed in his direction but I wasn't mad at him. I was simply glad that he felt as good as I did when I was around him.

~ Chapter 15 ~

The streets were silent as we strolled back to our apartment hand in hand. The air was warm and I felt even warmer after the flushing experience that I had just encountered. Sexual energy had been racing through my veins all night and I was both physically and mentally drained. It was only the support of Nelson that kept me stable as my feet floated across the dusty ground back through the strip. It was late and only a few shops were still open on our way back. A red and white sign illuminated the path in front of us and my stomach leapt at the sight of the 24-hour fast food sign in the distance. I needed to soak up all of the drinks that I had at the bar and our saucy action had worked up an appetite inside of me.

"I could really do with some fried chicken and French fries right now…" I hinted in Nelson's direction.

"Do you want to stop at the food shop over there?" he asked me signalling towards the 24-hour restaurant. And I immediately smiled towards him.

"If you wouldn't mind, I'm starving!" I amplified the truth a little but I couldn't resist the taste of a takeaway after a good night out.
"Sure. I don't mind. Besides, I'm dying to use a restroom," he added. I looked at him sideways.
"Restroom? But you can go anywhere?" That was the beauty of being a guy; they didn't need to worry where they released themselves.
"We can't do EVERYTHING anywhere…" he emphasised. And after a moment, I caught on to the subliminal message that he was trying to send.
"Fair enough," I ended it there. I didn't want any disturbing images spoiling my perfect picture of him.

As we arrived outside, a few empty red and white benches and tables stood before us. They were low and shiny. A sloping roof hung above, protecting the furniture from the harsh weathers of the Caribbean. As I looked into the shop, I could see only a single staff member serving a sizable queue of customers. Both the customers and the lone member of staff looked frustrated and I began to grit my teeth at the sight of it.
"I'll wait here," I told him knowing how thin my patience would be if I attempted to stand in that queue.
"That's cool. I'm just going to head to the restroom then I'll order us some food," he disclosed before disappearing into the shop. I sighed a sigh of relief as I plonked myself onto the rock-hard stools. Though they were not comfortable, they gave some respite to my howling dogs.

"Yo! You good?" A voice called from across the road. I looked up in curiosity, searching for who the comment was aimed at. The only people I could see were a small group of guys leaning on some metal fencing bars across the way. I couldn't make out who they were speaking to so I gave up and continued to stretch out the pain in my swollen feet.

"Yes, pink dress on the bench. I'm talking to you!" I looked up in the direction of the group of boys again. I was the only one wearing anything near to pink so I knew that he had to be talking to me. Silently, I sniggered at his ignorance between pink and nude as I rolled my eyes to myself. *Typical.* I thought to myself. However, I didn't want to show any disrespect so I openly responded with a polite thumbs up and a smile. They were so far away from me that I couldn't actually identify which guy I was signalling to.

"Can I talk to you for a minute?" he bellowed from over the street. I looked around for Nelson's whereabouts but he was nowhere to be seen.

"Yeah. Why not?" I didn't see the harm in having a friendly conversation whilst I waited for Nelson to release his load.

"Come nuh..." He beckoned but I was too tired to move.

"My feet are hurting but you are welcome to join me." I hollered back. Without hesitation, he jumped off of the fence and bounced right over to me.

He wore thick cornrows in his hair which dangled down to his broad shoulders and his skin was patched cream and brown. As he got closer, I noticed that his skin darkened around his joints and the rest appeared to be raw as if he had been bleaching his skin or he had eczema. Despite his skin condition, he walked with confidence and his eyes were deep and dark. One of his hands were tucked comfortably into the front of his jeans whilst the other one swayed freely. He kept a constant smirk on his face, as if his thoughts ran deeper than his actions. His eyebrows were well groomed whilst his beard was not. His full beard coiled down his face lengthening the appearance of his chin. I gave him a welcoming smile as he neared my bench.

"You 'ave a beautiful smile you nuh." He wagged his index finger towards me. "What are you doing sitting here all alone?" His fragrance was overpowering and he smelt phenomenal.

"Thanks. I'm just waiting for my friend who's getting us food," I responded, not giving much away but his smile widened nonetheless. It revealed his gold tooth which sat at the side of his mouth. There was something manly about a gold tooth which I found slightly attractive.

"Oh, I see. Me like yuh accent still you nuh. Weh you frum?" he asked. I squinted at him momentarily, trying to decipher his thick accent.

"I'm from London," I finally replied.

"Oh, so you're a bri'ish girl then…" he jived mocking my accent.

"Yes, although I think I love Jamaica a lot more." I laughed.

"So do you like a cuppa tea with your biscuit?" he continued. I could tell that he enjoyed amusing himself with his attempt at a British accent. He sounded more like someone from the film *Oliver* than anyone I had actually come across in my lifetime.

"Occasionally…" I replied as I thought for a while with a smile on my face. Briefly, I rationalised my liking of tea and biscuits; considering whether it was because I was British or because they tasted so good.

"So yuh mussi rich wid dem bri'ish pounds don't? Gimme yuh purse nuh." He smirked and I laughed at his jovial banter. As I caught contact with him, his eyes fixed with mine. It was a look so intense that I could feel him burning through me. I smiled back awkwardly to lighten the mood.

"You're funny!" I replied, forcibly baring all teeth.

"Mi look like seh mi a bus joke wid yuh?" His voice deepened as he spoke slowly and quietly, "Mi seh, gimme your purse…" his wide-leg stance fixed as his eyes bored their way through me. My mouth began to dry and I quickly scanned the restaurant for Nelson. He was still nowhere to be seen. I attempted to read the bearded man, unsure of his sarcasm.

"And why would I do that?" I held my breath as I tested the waters and awaited a response. His stomach forced a short but quick breath through his nostrils as he smirked.

"Because I get what I want…" His eerily calm voice confused me. I waited for a moment or two to see if he would burst into laughter, but he didn't. My breathing rate deepened. Thoughts dashed back and forth through my head as I attempted to think of the best way to react. Though part of me wanted to comply a bigger part of me wanted to stand up for myself.

"Well, you're not taking what's not yours," I bravely responded. My mind focused on all of the precious possessions I had inside of my purse. It contained all of my personal details. My address, my money, my passport. His jaw clenched tightly as he reached into the waist of his pants and my heart plunged into my chest. I froze, not knowing whether to hand my purse over there and then or to hold onto it tighter. I questioned whether there was a way to slip my belongings out of my purse without him noticing before I handed it over.

"You good?" A voice called from behind. It was Nelson's. He walked out of the glass door and towards me. I forced a smile with gritted teeth, trying to convince him that everything was okay but he didn't seem to buy it. He came over, empty-handed sizing up the two-toned man. He hadn't even bought the food yet. He could tell something was up. The man's dark eyes shot to where the voice was coming from and my heart beat intensified.

"Listen. Nuh budduh come innah my argument," he hissed at Nelson with his hand still in his pants. I longed for him to release his hand from whatever he was holding onto but he didn't.

"Her argument is my argument." Nelson's hand cupped his fist as he gesticulated for emphasis. "So what's the problem?" He stepped towards the bleached, bearded man, slightly towering over him. I watched speechless as Nelson stood face to face with him. He stared down into the guy's deep, dark eyes. I had never seen Nelson become so protective but the man remained firm in his position.

"Come owttah mi face bwoy," he growled at Nelson. His head edged forward as he spoke. The pulse in my chest began to quicken as my thoughts focused on his hand that clutched on to whatever was in his waist. There was no way I would allow Nelson to get shot or stabbed in my defence.

"Just leave it Nelson. It's nothing." I found my voice. Whilst I was glad Nelson had come to my defence, I didn't want antagonise the situation.

"No…" Nelson smirked. "I want to know what the problem is…" He spoke to me but his eyes were fixed on him. My eyes closed as I shook my head in dismay.

"Move from me. Now." The man's nose began to twitch whilst he spoke towards Nelson. His eyes looked as raw as his skin. I could tell he was becoming more frustrated.

"Why? What you gonna do?" Nelson puffed his chest, marking his territory. No matter what I said, I could tell that there was no way that he was backing down.

The two-toned man looked Nelson down then up and began to smirk. His head turned to his friends momentarily before he reached his hand out of his pants and my eyes widened in fear.

Bang!

Before I could do anything, he had launched his fist towards Nelson's face and pounded it right into him. Nelson's jaw began to misalign as his head was forced backwards. My heart clenched. Eyes red, Nelson was enraged. He growled as he held his hot cheek then instantaneously blazed him in the stomach. Nelson grit his teeth as his blow catapulted the man into the air. I could tell that he was now taking the situation personally.

"Ugghh!" The guy coughed from the backlash of the blow. He swung for Nelson again. My whole body stiffened. But Nelson dodged out of the way leaving his fist to fly through the air and into the distance. Taking advantage of his wobbling stance, Nelson battered his head with a series of punches that caused it to jerk back and forth between each bang. Saliva swung from his mouth as he tried to regain his balance. I couldn't move. He attempted to fight back but the force from Nelson's blows were too intense. Although I was stricken with fear, my eyes gleamed at the sight of Nelson taking him down.

As Nelson continued to pound him, the man's jaw wobbled and smacked against the pavement. I could see a glint in Nelson's eyes as his rage relentlessly focused on teaching this brute a lesson. There was no stopping him and I began to worry as the guy became defenceless against Nelson.

"Just leave him Nelson! He's not worth it!" I called to him but he completely ignored me. His rage had possessed him so much that he had not even realised that the guy's friends were heading in our direction. As his friends paced over, they were hollering aggressively at the boys. I couldn't understand what they were saying but I felt a sense of relief that someone would be strong enough to drag Nelson off of their friend and save what was left of him.

Buff!

Buff!

Buff!

My jaw fell to the floor as they barked at Nelson and flew punches towards his face. My chest restricted as I watched him fall to the floor. I could see Nelson using his arms as a desperate attempt to shield himself. "Stop!" I yelled but they continued and streams of tears ran out of my eyes as I clenched my purse powerlessly. Four men on one guy; there was no way that this could be fair.

Buff!

Buff!

Bang!

"Please stop!" I begged. Nelson's body bounced off of the pavement as they launched their feet into him. But my screaming was like white noise to them as they repeatedly kicked him in his stomach. Shrieks of pain blurted out of his mouth as they stomped on him like a tomato. He needed help. Something had to be done. My sobbing volumised… "PLEASE!" I yelled as I attempted to drag them away from him. But their force shot me backwards onto the fence. Crowds of people came out of the fast food restaurant as the raucous exploded. Seeing how helpless I was, the people started to shout at the group of men "Lef him nuh man!" one guy ordered. But they continued until blood splurted out of Nelson's mouth as it collided with the floor. "That will teach you not to fuck with us!" they shouted as they paced down the streets and into the darkness.

They left Nelson, helplessly coughing on the ground as he tried to recover from the pain. I lurched onto him grabbing his swollen face as the tears rolled down my eyes. I couldn't believe my eyes. Both his eyelids had tripled in size with one eye distinctly redder than the other. Bloodshot. I held onto him as he tried to spit his blood onto the pavement. It was considerably hard for him to do taking into account the growing size of his bottom lip. His clothes were dishevelled and his body felt limp. Anxiously, I searched his body for wounds but found none. Though he flinched when I felt his waist, there was nothing that I could physically see. His waist felt tender and I feared that he had broken a bone or two.

"We need to get you to a hospital!" I wailed as I held him in my arms.
"Don't … worry…. I'm fine." His voice rasped as he spoke. I shook my head in disapproval as the tears streamed down my face.
"How can you be fine? You can barely speak!" I cried.
"Neither can you…" he coughed whilst he attempted to laugh. Though I could see that he was making light of the situation, it looked so painful to watch him like that. A man rushed over with a bottle of water in his hand.
"Let him sip this," he ordered as he handed me the drink. A small group of people helped me to lift him so that his body was more upright. His body still flopped to one side. As I lifted the bottle to Nelson's mouth, he began spitting it out. A diluted puddle of blood formed on the ground.
"Stop being hard-headed and swallow it!" I urged. His face winced as he swallowed.
"Are you in pain?" I foolishly asked. I knew the answer the moment the words left my mouth. Somehow, I wanted him to reassure me.

"Of course I am… but it's all good… I just… need… to… sleep it… off…" he swallowed air in between each word. I huffed at his stubbornness. I wasn't quite sure how he thought that he could sleep off a swollen face. "This isn't England. We don't just rush to hospital over any sneeze or cough. It's not free." His words sounded weak. I wiped the tears from my nose.

"But this isn't just any type of cough!" I wheezed as I spoke but I understood his position. He didn't think it was life-threatening enough. "Just tell me, can you move all of your fingers and toes?" I urged for reassurance.
"Trust me… everything is in working order…" He smiled weakly at me. "Just take me back to the apartment...Please," he begged. His big, puppy dog eyes were bargaining with me. I had no choice but to follow his wishes.

* * *

That night, I couldn't sleep a wink. My mind was swollen with worry and fear for Nelson's safety. His cheeks twitched as he rested and I could feel his pain. A pulse strengthened in my chest as I watched him sleep. It pounded in time to his breathing which was heavier than usual. His chest wheezed piercingly with every breath that he took. Buckets of sweat dripped from his body and soaked the mattress below him. A wet patch marked the outline of his body like a dead corps but I prayed for the best. I wasn't as religious as I used to be but I felt powerless in this situation. I was convinced that only a higher force was capable of saving his wilted soul and my dying faith. Riddled with guilt, I tried to block out the negative thoughts that brainwashed me to believe that it was all my fault. But they were too strong. Whispering voices caused me to question my every move that night. *Why did we even stop for food? Why didn't I wait inside? Why did I even invite that guy over?*

The only reasons that I could think of were purely selfish so I couldn't help but blame myself.

I prayed my hardest that he would make it through the night and not slip into a coma. My mouth dried quickly after my intense bargaining with God and I longed for a glass of water. My eyes followed his every movement as I sat up to drink. I tried to convince myself that everything had happened for a reason but for some reason that train of thought was hard to swallow. I only hoped that I would learn a massive lesson from the situation so that I could never see him in such pain again. As the moon moved through the sky, I laid beside him only taking my eyes off of him to blink. Time dragged as I kept a close eye on him, patiently waiting for him to achieve consciousness once more.

As the sun rose, the pulse that was in my chest crept into my skull causing my body functioning to shut down. I was exhausted. My eyes were red raw but I was determined to stay awake until Nelson opened his eyes again. I stroked his head gently as I laid beside him, whispering my apologies into the atmosphere. Though he showed no sign of consciousness, I longed for him to forgive me.

"You don't stop talking in your sleep do you?" His voice croaked as he spoke his first words of the day. Slowly, he peeled his puffy eyelids apart and focused on me. "Good morning beautiful." He smiled weakly at me and automatically, I smiled back at him. I pressed my lips deeply into his forehead and he began to flinch.

"How are you feeling?" I asked relieved at the sight of his waking eyes.
"Like I've been hit by a truck..." He yawned as he stretched his body outwards. "You don't look too righteous yourself." As he cross examined me, I noticed that the redness in his eye had worsened and had spread across his entire eyeball. Though it pained me to look at him like this, I was glad to hear him talking again. "I know. I've been up worrying about you all night," I replied.
"For what? You don't need to worry about me. I'm a fighter," he reassured me but my eyes rolled in disbelief nonetheless. "You need to sleep Raven."
"I will," I replied.
"Don't worry. You can rest your head while I drive us back to your hotel." He attempted to stroke my cheek but I moved away.
"Nelson, there's no way you are driving back in your condition. You can barely see out of those swollen eyelids of yours." I asserted myself.
"I can see just fine. It's just a little bruising." He tried to convince me but I wasn't buying any of it this time round.
"Listen, I am not letting you drive me back whilst you are in this state. Your body is in shock and so is mine. We both need to rest!" I spoke firmly and he retreated.
"Okay, I hear you."
"We need to take a taxi back," I added. "You'll have to get your car another time."

"Yes ma'am!" He saluted me weakly with a mocking look in his eyes. I could see that he was in no mood to argue with me. Though I knew his feeble mood was mostly due to his state, I appreciated the fact that he was letting his pride go for once.

I tossed back the sheets in search for some food.
"You must be ravenous," I half murmured to Nelson. I was hungry but Nelson's body must have been starving after all of the trauma that he had been through. I felt it was my duty to look after him as he had been nothing but protective over me the night before. As I rifled through the rose-wooden cupboards, I found nothing. The cupboards were completely bare. I huffed in annoyance. "Let's get you ready so that we can get some food on the way back." He stared back at me helplessly and my level of guilt almost quadrupled. I headed towards him. "Thank you for last night." I embraced him apologetically.
"No problem. There was no way that I was going to let that guy get away with troubling you."
"I was petrified. I don't know what I would've done if you weren't there. Seriously, I truly appreciate it." My embrace tightened briefly before releasing him.

Nelson called the taxi whilst I packed our things and not long after, the driver arrived. We sat in the back seat of the taxi hand in hand but we barely spoke a word to each other. On our journey back, my eyes grew heavy quite quickly as I rested my head against the car window. I slept for the entire journey barely noticing any of the humps in the road.

~ Chapter 16 ~

It had been days since I had spoken to Nelson and the days seemed like weeks without him. I sat by the pool alone, people watching, whilst the blazing sun blessed my glowing skin. The water splashed as the children dived and the laughter passed through the people like a contagious bug. Somehow, I was immune. Though I was in the most perfect place, I couldn't enjoy it. The only joy I received was from the taste of my strawberry daiquiri as the slush slid down my throat but I couldn't even enjoy that without my thoughts drifting towards Nelson. No matter how much I filled my cup, there still was an emptiness inside of me without his presence. He hadn't been at work since his incident and I knew that he had to be recovering. But I longed to hear from him. Only he could fill the void in me.

I reached for phone in my handbag to search for his number. *"Where have you been? I need you."* I typed then quickly deleted it. Though I missed him badly, I didn't want to sound selfish. *"Hey, are you okay?"* That sounded a lot more fitting. I could see that he had read my message but he had not yet replied. I reclined on the lounger as I awaited his response.

"Feeling much better now. How are you?" he responded and my heart skipped with joy. It was the simplest of messages yet it made me feel so giddy inside.

"I'm good. I was just relaxing when you crossed my mind. I thought I'd check up on you." I played it cool. Though I wanted to express my burning desire to speak to him, I could not tell how he felt about me. I was curious to know whether he had blamed the whole situation on me and I wouldn't have blamed him if he did. I wouldn't want to have with contact someone who had gotten me beaten black and blue either.

"I've missed you too. I've just been recovering." He read right through me, in spite of my depiction of breeziness.

"You've missed me have you? I suppose, I have too," I jovially responded. *"Will you be back at work any time soon?"* I hinted.

"No. I have the week off. But I am feeling a lot better," he replied. Selfishly, my smile sunk. Whilst I was glad that he was recovering, I did miss seeing him around the hotel.

"Thank you for looking after me the other night," he wrote shortly after.

"No. Thank you! I don't know what I would have done without you that day." I couldn't believe how humble he was being. *"I owe you one,"* I reminded him.

"Seriously, I really appreciate your support, so does my wife." My cheeks dropped. I hated the thought of her, especially when he was away from me. He began typing again. *"She would like to meet you."* My heart froze, *"to thank you personally;"* so did my breathing.

"*What?*" I couldn't believe my eyes.

"*If it weren't for you, who knows what would have happened to me. She respects that,*" he wrote but I wasn't quite sure why she would want to meet me; the girl who happily slept with her husband.

"*What exactly did you tell her? I'm not sure that I'm comfortable with that,*" I replied.

"*I just told her that I got into a fight and you made sure I was okay when I was weak.*"

"*And…?*"

"*That's all. She thinks it was really charitable of you to nurse me when I was sick and take me under your wing.*" He skirted around the truth and I giggled inside.

"*Very charitable indeed…*" I shot back, one eyebrow raised. "*But does she know who I am?*"

"*Yes. The girl who looked after me when I got beaten by a group of strangers.*" His answers were vague but I read between the lines.

"*My wife insists that you come over for dinner. Will you come?*" he asked. I thought for a moment.

"*I don't think I should.*" I couldn't bear to dine with the other woman, though in actual fact, that was my role.

"*Why? There's no harm in it. She just wants to thank you. Can't you do it for me, please?*" I wasn't sure how awkward it would be eating dinner at his but I felt obliged to. Not only did I long to see Nelson again but my guilt coerced me to comply. Though it seemed that his wife was none the wiser about our relationship, I was curious to meet her. I was intrigued about the type of female that would be so relaxed about her husband's liaisons.

"O.K." I replied hesitantly. But it was too late. The message had sent.

"Great! I'll send a taxi for you at 8!" he wrote back and I could almost feel his excitement through the phone. Though I was nowhere near as excited as he was, I was most definitely intrigued.

~ Chapter 17 ~

"*Your taxi will be at the front in 5 minutes.*" My heart plunged as I read his message. Despite the countless hours I had to get ready, nothing could have prepared me for this. I never would have believed that I would ever be in this type of this situation but this guy had me smitten. I was now doing all kinds of things that I never would have done before but this had topped them all. Coming face to face with the other woman, incognito; that was nothing short of a MI5 mission; I just hoped that it wouldn't be impossible.

My hands began to clam up as I gathered the last of my necessities to put in my handbag. I wanted to be well prepared. I had my hotel key, my phone, my lip gloss and my pointed tweezers, just in case. My tweezers were my secret weapon, in the event that I needed an emergency pluck or a sharp weapon to stab. Though my thoughts seemed extreme, my paranoia always heightened in situations where I was entering the unknown, almost involuntary. This situation was one of them. It came as a blessing and a curse; my paranoia. Whilst it allowed me to be organised and ready for any situation, my overthinking also crippled my sense of spontaneity. Like a terminal disease, it viciously killed my wild side and froze my sense of ease. Nelson was the first guy in a long time who was able to encourage me to let my guard down and it felt so right allowing things to 'just happen' when I was around him.

Though I had started to build trust for Nelson, I felt the sudden urge to protect myself knowing that I was going to meet his wife. Whilst he insisted that she did not know my real identity, something in the back of my mind also insisted that I kept myself safe. Bag in hand, I headed through the lobby and towards the front entrance. My head lowered and my eyes shifted as I scrambled through in shame. Eyes burned through me like tracking lasers. I felt hot, almost as if everyone knew my dirty secret. They knew that I was brazen enough to go and meet the wife of the man I was sleeping with. The mass of people that crowded in the lobby made it feel as though the walls were closing in on me but I knew that it was my heightened paranoia mixed with my guilt that made me feel so exposed.

"Stop being silly Raven. It'll be fine," I convinced myself as I stepped out into the open air. I inhaled the deepest of breaths and exhaled it with just as much force. As I tried to calm myself down, I continued my confidence-boosting internal monologue. But

unsurprisingly, it seemed harder than before to convince myself that this was okay and I was going to be okay.

"I'm only going for a dinner. She just wants to thank me."

"For fucking her husband!" My guilty conscience interrupted. I tried to shake the negative thoughts.

"I am friendly. I am wise. I am confident." I repeated to myself over and over again as I waited by the security box. And every time I felt a negative thought creeping in, I repeated my mantra even louder in my head until I had dulled the sound of my guilty conscience.

"Raven?" An assertive voice called from a large, silver car. A black and white checkered strip wrapped round the middle of the car like a ribbon. Unlike the other vehicles, he held a black and yellow sign on his roof and I noticed that his registration plate was red. I was almost certain this was my taxi.

"Yes. That's me." I stepped forward, forcing a smile to emerge on my face.

"Are you heading to the Tannerman residence?" he confirmed.

"Yes I am." My smile clenched slightly as reality hit me.

Within moments, he had stepped out to open the car door for me and I took comfort in the backseat. I placed my bag on my lap and hugged it closely to my stomach, like a pillow. The closer I held it, the more comfort I felt about what I was doing and what I was about to do. He smiled as he shut the car door and headed to the driver's seat.

"So, you're heading to Rose Hall?" he confirmed as he pulled his seat belt over him and forced it into the buckle.
"I am," I replied, half questioning and half confirming him. It was at that moment, that it had dawned on me that I didn't actually know where I was going. I didn't actually know where Nelson lived. It made me wonder. What else didn't I know about him? My paranoia began to creep back as I questioned how much I could actually trust someone who hadn't told me where they lived.

As I stared through the window, I couldn't help but cast my mind back to the guys I had met in the past and had an absolute blast with. One in particular, Andre. I remember meeting him for the first time in my car outside his house. I had met him on an internet dating website and when I saw him, he was exactly my type on paper. He was tall, dark and full of beard. A quirky beard too. Every time I met up with him, he had dyed the mid-strip of his beard a different colour and blow dried it to perfection. He had an innocent glint in his eyes though his mouth was full of flirt and sexual innuendos. His basketballer body was to die for and we shared a similar taste in music. Week after week, I would drive to his house and we would sit outside and talk in my car. Every time that we met, he would invite me in and I would say no. Mainly because I was so petrified of the fact that I had met him on the internet and I was worried about what could've happened to me if I stepped inside his house. Somehow, I felt safety in my car. We got on a like house on fire yet he never knew where I lived and I had never been inside his house. Eventually, our relationship fizzled out as I refused to take it to the next level, even though our bond had strengthened. I had known Andre for months but only known Nelson for a week though it felt like much longer. In the grand scheme of things, I had realised that it wasn't that bad that I didn't know where he lived.

"It's real nice 'round Rose Hall. Really nice." The driver winked at me through the windscreen mirror and I smiled back politely. "Do you like it up there?" he asked, eager to make conversation. A small part of me didn't want to reveal much of my ignorance to the driver so I decided to steer the conversation away from me.

"Mmm… Do you know many people in Rose Hall?" Though I loathed small talk, somehow, I always found myself involved in it.

"Not really. That place there is for the highty tighties." He laughed. "I live downtown."

"Really?" My interested tone sounded convincing.

"Very different from Rose Hall. That's where the real ghetto youths squander. Everyone has to work hard to butter their bread down there," he continued.

"And you don't think that they work hard in Rose Hall?" I goaded him for more.

"Well, not really. It's a different type of hard. They don't really like to get their hands dirty around there if you know what I mean." He smirked to himself and my chin raised towards him but this time, with genuine interest. I was intrigued to know how well off one had to be to live in that area.

"Would you ever like to live there?" I asked.

"Ha! In my dreams, maybe. But for real, I like to be surrounded by real people. I don't think I would ever fit in around there. As bad as it can be at night, I could never imagine myself moving from downtown." He stared nostalgically into the distance for a moment before engaging me again. "So I take it you're from England then? Whereabouts?" Somehow, he had steered the conversation back in my direction.

"I live in London," I replied.

"Oh, I have family that live near there, in Yorkshire?" he stated in an awful attempt to find common ground.

"Yeah... London is not that close to Yorkshire. It would probably take around 4 hours to drive there from my side of town." I laughed.

"So do you have family over here in Jamaica then?" he asked.

"Yeah."

"Is that who you're visiting?" he asked. My face flushed hot.

"Not quite. Just friends." My forced smile had reappeared.

"Well, I hope you're enjoying your time here…" He finished, almost sensing my awkwardness.

As he drove down the road, he gestured to the great plantation house that the area was named after. It was a grand house in the centre of a vast field with low cut lawn. A cemented path led straight from the sizable, black gates by the main road, right to the wide-set stairs by the house. It was an eye-catching property indeed. As I looked on in awe, I couldn't help but imagine all of the slaves that would have worked in the field for their masters in the sweltering sun. I was thankful that those days were over. As he drove off of the main road, he took us up a winding path that encircled the hills. From the bottom of the jerky hill to where we were headed, I noticed how the track began to change. Rough rubble had transformed into a smoother slab of tarmac. Grand, brick houses hid behind trees in a community that was levitated from the terrain. The driver began to slow as we reached the low, stone wall which led to a pair of big, black gates. I couldn't believe that Nelson lived in an area like this. The driver stepped out of the vehicle to press the buzzer.

All of a sudden, I had an overwhelming urge to pee. My nerves were getting the better of me. And as the gates extended, my bladder began to swell to what felt like more than twice of its capacity. I was keen to release. The taxi drove up the smoothed path which was neatly lined with stone walls and trimmed bushes. Palm trees grew on either side of the coral flight of stairs that led straight to the front entrance. And as we arrived at the double doors, a fair-skinned woman bounced down the steps to meet us. "Thank you very much!" She smiled at the driver as she handed him a few notes to cover the journey. "I'm sure that's more than enough." She winked as he counted the cash with an inerasable

grin on his face. "You must be Raven…" she turned to me with her hand extended towards mine.
"Yes. I am." I smiled awkwardly as I shook her hand.

As I looked at her, I couldn't help but notice the intrigued look in her sharp, blue eyes. It was quite profound. She was an absolutely stunning woman, slightly older than I was. She was probably nearing her forties but she wore her age well. I could tell that she was of a mixed heritage. She wore her soft curls in a bob that complimented her defined yet feminine jaw line. A light sprinkle of freckles sat on her high cheekbones and danced around her thick but shaped eyebrows. Her dark eyelashes swept across her eyelids, accentuating her crystal blue eyes. Though her lips were full, her body was slim and kept in good shape. "I'm Mara Tannerman, Nelson's wife. It's a pleasure to meet you." Her greeting was just as eloquent as her sense of style.
"You too," I cordially replied. Though it burned me to find that Nelson's wife was so drop-dead gorgeous. "I was wondering whether I could use your toilet? I've been holding tight my entire journey," I coyly asked.
"Of course. We wouldn't want you to be holding tight for much longer!" She laughed and I joined in nervously. "I'll show you the way."

As we walked through the marbled foyer, there were a number of dark wooden doors and a winding flight of stairs that led to the second floor. The bannister ran all the way along the staircase and across the landing of the second level, making it appear quite open. However, she escorted me to a door on the left of the ground floor landing which led to me to a granite embellished washroom. "Thanks" I uttered before diving in. As I lifted my dress to sit down, a burst of relief left my body. I sat momentarily, taking it all in. Mara seemed like such a beautiful woman with a beautiful home. I didn't understand why Nelson would even dream of being with anyone else. However, she was slightly older than us so she probably saw things differently. And maybe her body felt different, making him lust for the younger vagina. Though I couldn't quite get my head around their agreement, I was happy to reap the benefits of it, even if it was unbeknownst to her.

After I had washed up, I checked myself in the wall encompassing mirror that faced me. It had been a while since I had seen Nelson and I wanted to look the part. I was apprehensive to know how well he looked and whether his swelling had subsided. Either way, it didn't matter as I was keen to see him regardless of his looks.

A humble looking woman awaited me as I stepped out of the washroom. She was dressed discreetly from her neck to her knees and her twists were neatly pinned down to her head.
"Your dinner is waiting to be served. Please follow me." She ushered as she took the lead down the hallway. I was astounded. *Help? Nelson lived with help?* Anyone that could afford to hire help

clearly had extra cash lying around. It didn't make sense to me. I didn't understand why Nelson would be working as bar staff in a hotel and drive a rusty, white car if he lived in a house like this.

It was a plush house indeed. The hallways were triple the size of the ones in my 1-bedroom flat. They were wide enough for two elephants to walk down with ease. Expensive and eye-catching art pieces hung from walls and a decorated the hallway. The double glazed sliding doors at the end of the hallway led to their spacious back yard. It was home to a vast spread of greenery and a decent sized pool. They seemed to have it all.

"Right this way." The help pointed as she opened one of the doors to the right of the double glazed wall. There they were, seated on a round table in the centre of the dining room. It was large enough to seat eight people. Yet there were only three of us. As I entered the room, my eyes met with his and I noticed his glint as I smiled politely at him. Though he wasn't completely back to optimum health, his teeth still shined and his dimple was just as endearing. The redness in his eye had reduced substantially along with his bruising.

"Come. Sit." Mara gestured to me. She spoke with a magnetic tone that was hard to ignore. "Thank you for helping my husband. We're both really grateful."

"No problem. My conscience would have eaten me alive if I had left him there in such a weak state," I said as I sat down two spaces away from both of them. "I had recognised him from the

hotel, so I had to help him back to his friend's. How are you feeling now?" I turned towards Nelson.
"Still sore in places but much better. Thank you," he replied in such a dignified manner. His behaviour seemed quite different to what I was used to. I deliberated whether the pain he had experienced had made him a little more reserved.
"He'll be as right as rain in a couple of days. Never you mind." She shrugged off his pity party.
"You have a lovely place," I mentioned as my eyes scoped the room.
"Thanks. We've worked hard to get it to where it is now," she responded rather proudly.
"Really? How long has it taken you?" I asked intrigued.
"Just over eighteen months but it was well worth the wait." It must have cost them a lot of money to get their home to look so sophisticated, I thought.
"What do you do?" I asked.
"Oh, what don't I do?" She laughed. "I'm into all sorts but my first love is my art exhibition. I collect fabulous pieces from all over and sell them to those who are looking for something unique. They always want something that they know others can't have," she divulged.
"Well, don't we all!" I added sharing a quick glance at Nelson. I could see him smiling to himself out of his wife's view.
"The majority do but I've found that when you give, you get a lot more in return," she remarked as she gestured to her home.

"And you work in the hotel? As bar staff?" I was curious about Nelson's position.

"Yes. It keeps him grounded," she answered for him, "Besides, who wants their husband slobbering around the house all day?" She laughed casually. "So what do you do with yourself then?"

"Oh, I'm an accountant. Boring, I know but it pays the bills." I smiled.

"So what do you do to make your life more interesting?" she asked and my cheeks grew rosy. If I had mentioned the first thing that came to my mind, she probably wouldn't have taken a liking to it despite how open Nelson had made her seem.

"Oh, not much. A holiday here and there but nothing too wild." I thought a generalisation was the best way to tackle that kind of question and she seemed fairly convinced by my response. "I must say, you have beautiful eyes. It's quite rare to see a woman of your complexion with eyes so blue. Does it run in your family?" I asked in diversion.

"Not as far I know. My dad was Irish but my mum was as dark as you. She had dark eyes too," she replied.

"Oh, so did your dad have blue eyes?" I probed.

"Not really. But it's hard to tell what will happen with throwback genes." She laughed. "So where are you from then?"

"My parents are Jamaican but I was born in England."

"England… I lived there for a while. Which part do you come from?" she asked and my eyes brightened as I found common ground with her.

"London."

"Oh, I wasn't too far from there. I lived in Manchester." As she spoke I began to smirk to myself. Manchester was nowhere near London. I found it quite comical that both her and my taxi driver had made such wild statements.

"Why were you living in England?" I inquired.

"I moved there after my mother died." Her face began to harden. I paused, unsure of how she felt about her situation and whether I should continue the conversation. An awkward silence swept across the room. After a while, I made an attempt to casually continue our discourse.

"I'm sorry to hear about your mother."

"It's okay. It's a part of life." She rose her cheeks in an attempt to smile and I returned her gesture.

"Yeah, I suppose. And you ended up back in Jamaica? That's not usually the choice for those who leave the island?"

"It's a long story but in the end it was just too cold and I missed the Jamaican food!" She laughed as she breezed past my question.

"Ahh, here it is!" Mara boasted in delight as her help brought in an array of dishes. Mackerel rundown, curried goat, brown-stewed chicken, rice and peas, steamed vegetables and fried plantain. It was enough food to feed the five thousand. She encouraged us to dive in but I only took a modest plateful. We ate, we spoke, we drank and my every whim was catered for. As Nelson's wife chattered on, I noticed how different he was around her. So quiet. He barely spoke at all. I was curious as to how he felt with me being around his wife. Though it was his idea for me to come round, he seemed so introverted. Yet, she had made me feel so comfortable that I almost felt guilty about my rendezvous with Nelson.

“You must stay the night," Mara insisted using her magnetic tone once more.

“No. I don’t think I should but thank you for offering.” I turned to her then to Nelson. He stared back at me, with his eyebrow slightly raised in amusement.

“Of course you should. Nothing beats a comfortable stay in a family home. Surely, you must get lonely staying by yourself in the hotel.” Her compelling voice strengthened. “You can stay in the guest room at the top of the stairs. That’s the least we could do. Isn’t that right Nelly?” She turned to him with a steady look in her eyes.

“Of course," he agreed with her. I could tell that their minds were already made up; her’s in particular. She wasn’t taking no for an answer and it didn’t hurt sleeping only a stone throw away from Nelson; down the corridor to be exact. A small smile crept onto my face.

“Okay," I agreed and she embraced her hands in delight.

~ Chapter 18 ~

My feet felt light and my head giddy as I stumbled to the ensuite bathroom of their guestroom. The array of drinks I'd been given at dinner had put me in a fluffy mood and made the simplest tasks seem as though they needed the highest level of coordination to be completed. I fumbled for the light in the bathroom. And as the light flickered on, my eyes focused in astonishment. I could tell that it wasn't just any standard room, it was guest- ready. It was complete with towels, soap and a toothbrush. The entire room felt like a home away from home but much better than my own. Everything seemed so clean and shiny.

As I plumped my bottom onto the porcelain toilet seat, a rush of whizz came out of me, making my body feel even lighter than before. It was the sense of relief I had been waiting for after the charade I had kept up at the dinner table. Though it was quite laborious in my light headed state, I made sure that I wiped myself and then the toilet seat so that everything was left just as it was found. The bathroom seemed too good to be touched; almost unworthy of me. As I went to wash my hands, I caught a glimpse of my eyes in the mirror; very happy indeed. My pores were wide open and my lips were full of vibration; tipsiness at its finest. I gave myself a quick splash to freshen up and it helped for all of five seconds.

A good night's sleep was just what I needed. I began to strip off and slip on the night dress that Mara had left on the king-sized bed for me. It was a little small on me because Mara had a slimmer frame than I had but I was too tired to care. I flung back the sheets and crawled right in. Though it felt slightly odd sleeping down the hallway from Nelson, it felt good to stay in such a homely room with a comfortable bed. I reached for my phone before settling in.

"Goodnight xx." I sent a cheeky text to Nelson before turning the bedside lamp off. I got a small rush from messaging him knowing that we were in the same vicinity.

"Sweet Dreams cutie pie," he wrote back and my feet began twiddle as I read his message. My eyes shut with a pleasant smile on my face and I rolled my cheek into the pillow to get comfortable. With one leg slightly out of the covers, I rested my stomach onto the memory foam mattress. I placed my hands close to my head as my cheeks grew heavier and I began to fall asleep.

It was probably one of my easier sleeps as the bed was so inviting. Egyptian cotton wrapped around me like a fluffy gown and the duck-feathered pillows felt as soft as a cloud. The room was the perfect temperature, thanks to the air conditioning and it was so silent that I could have heard a pin drop. It made a massive difference to the incessant sound of grasshoppers croaking outside the window at night. It was no wonder that sleep engulfed me so quickly.

But as I sunk deeper into the bed, I felt the tender stroke of hands. First on my shoulders; thumbs rubbed deep circles around the back of my neck forcing me to sink deeper into the mattress. My mind drifted between dream and wake state. I didn't notice at first but my head began to flounce in delight. Then the strokes began to explore my back. Fingertips twirled and whirled with conviction, with meaning. There was only one person who had the ability to make me feel so weak and I began to smile in the sheets whilst the pleasure from those relentless fingertips had their wicked way with me. As I lay on my back, I couldn't help but bite my lip at the cheeky nature of it all. The last thing I expected was a visit in the night.

My night dress began to rise higher and higher, giving more leverage for my back to be stroked. My hair raised on end as the silk night dress brushed past my every fibre. Being the polite guest that I was, I eased my hips then my chest up, making it easier for my dress to rise. The strokes made me looser and wetter. My back was complemented with kisses. Slow, sensual kisses that travelled all the way down my spine.

"Mmm…" I let out a groan in delight as his glorious tongue slipped through my crack. It was an oddly pleasurable sensation. I had never had a tongue anywhere near my bottom before but this felt electrifying. With a tight grip on my cheeks that tongue was buried deep inside, levering forwards and backwards. It sent a sensational, prickly vibration underneath my skin. As the strokes grew more intense, I longed for my cherry to be tasted.

My back began to arch, lifting my hips higher off the bed. I tried to curve my clitoris on to his warm mouth but somehow it just couldn't connect. I collapsed on to the bed in frustration. But the grab on my thighs reassured me that he knew what I was looking for. I was eased onto my front and my legs were spread apart under the sheets. My eyes spun back in my head in anticipation until I felt that wet tongue all over me once more. I inhaled deeply as my clitoris was massaged with all the tongue base I could fathom. I had never experienced a pressure so intense. My legs spread further in delight as I was devoured like a dessert.

Creeeaaakk.

A sound forced my head to shoot straight over to the door which was slightly a jar. My legs were held firmly apart; tongue still lapping underneath the sheets. But as I looked, I saw nothing. Just a silent hallway. No movement. Nothing. I tried to focus for a while but the intense strokes that seemed to feel even more so now made my eyelids weak. My clitoris began to throb in delight, sending signals of sweetness directly to my brain. And then a sweet finger slipped inside my moistness, as smooth as a raindrop. My walls welcomed it like a fresh lick of paint. Then two fingers penetrated in and out of me as my clitoris danced swiftly in time with the relentless tongue motions.

My head arched backwards in bliss. As the finger penetration proceeded, I felt one, then two hands on my nipples. The fingers ran smoothly over both of my nipples back and forth. Back and forth as I was sucked and finger fucked. I was so overwhelmed in pleasure that my eyes began to water. *What was he doing to me?* Horniness heightened, I reached for his head to place a deep, wet kiss all over his lips. And as I reached forward, he embraced me with both arms, returning my need to be kissed but the tongue lapping continued underneath the sheets.

My eyes widened in shock.

"What the fuck Nelson?" I whispered with my hands still wrapped firmly around his head.

"It's okay," he whispered in between kisses, "Just lay back and enjoy." His hands returned to my bosoms encircling the meat of them tenderly. Though my head didn't know what to think, my body welcomed the sensation of my four pleasure points being stimulated simultaneously. Sparks rushed around my sexual triangle as I laid back in awe and I could not reject the pleasure of it all. I knew his wife was down there, but he was up here and I didn't care. Mara's fingers stroked over my lady-spot over and over whilst her tongue swirled round and round. My clitoris and

vaginal muscles began to pulsate in unison. First, lightly but as she continued, I could no longer take the quadruple levels of gratification that were being given to me. My pulsations strengthened. My moans intensified as my body began to levitate off of the bed. I was coming. Harder than ever before.
"Aaaahhh…" I groaned as my limbs began to spasm in joy. Joy leapt through my every fibre until my body came to a still; smiling like a Cheshire cat.

"You liked that didn't you?" Mara smirked as she bit her bottom lip. I was speechless. I was dripping and too horny to find words. She turned to Nelson "I want you to fuck her." My blinking doubled. I couldn't quite believe what I was hearing. Mara wanted her husband to fuck me in front of her. I knew they were in an open relationship but she was taking it to a whole other level. I didn't mind Nelson having his wicked way with me behind his wife's back but I didn't know how I felt about infidelity right in front of her face. Nelson glared at me smiling from one side of his mouth. His Mowgli smile always made me weak.

As he undid his robe, he looked at me for reassurance. His dick was steadfast. "Are you ready for this?" he whispered in my ear. My eyes widened before squinting in his direction. I didn't know what to make of the situation. My body was more than ready and so was his evidently. But my mind was unsure. I glanced over to

Mara and she raised an eyebrow in my direction. Though it was dark, I could sense the glow in her cheeks.
"Don't worry about me. I can see that you're horny. Go ahead," she goaded me using that magnetic tone. "What are you waiting for Nelson? Fuck her!" she gently ordered and Nelson withdrew his mighty sword.

Grabbing my legs, he dragged me to the end of the bed and readied himself to insert his cock. I lifted my hips towards him to ease his penetration. As he entered me, a force of delight shot through my veins.
"Mmmm…" I sighed as my eyes began to close.
"You like that don't you?" Mara whispered as Nelson continued to bury his shaft deep inside of me over and over. I opened my eyes momentarily. Mara smiled as she began to run her fingers then her tongue all over my breast. "This is how we say thank you around here…" she continued as she began licking my earlobe and I couldn't help but giggle. Nelson's chocolate chest huffed and puffed as he drove his way in and out of me. My hips moved in time with his, heightening the sensation of pleasure.

I felt a fullness inside of me when he shoved his penis all the way in; a sense of completion. And I quickly grew accustomed to the vision of Mara's lips all over my torso. Her blushed pink lips felt so gentle. Wherever her lips would go, her hands would follow, accentuating the feeling. My mouth made a perfect O when

Nelson changed his gear from drive to grind. His dick smoothed round my entire capsule, leaving no area untouched.

As he continued grinding, Mara's hand ran down my stomach towards my clitoris. She began to massage my cherry in time Nelson's rhythm. My body responded with rapture. Her smooth motion sent signals of bliss through my veins. My walls relaxed as he eased his penis onto them. I had never felt that amount of euphoria before. And as I looked at Mara, a rose-tinted glow surrounded her beauty. The shine from the sweat made her skin glisten in the dark. She looked absolutely stunning and what she was doing with her hands was making her even sexier. My eyes lingered on her for a moment. I couldn't believe that she was making me feel this way. I had never thought a female was sexy before but Mara had me yearning for more of her.

Nelson grabbed my hips and thrusted his whole length inside of me causing shots of pleasure to fire through my entire being. As he continued, I lurched my hands forward to get a feel of her. I wanted to feel Mara's whole body over mine but as I reached forward to touch her, she grabbed hold of my hands. She clasped them so tight that my circulation paused momentarily.

"Relax. Let me take control," she whispered as she forced my hands above my head before placing a soft kiss on my neck. Twisting her body around, she sat on my hands with her legs slightly straddled around my head. "Now that should keep you in check." She giggled as she began grinding her pussy all over them.

The more she grinded, the wetter she became. She rocked back and forth as Nelson slid in and out of me. I could feel her moistness all over my palm. The hornier she became, the more assertive she got. Forcing my hands into her vagina as her perked breasts hovered over my face. She smelt heavenly. I began to kiss her breasts as they brushed past my lips. As I kissed them, she began forcing my fingers into her deeper and deeper. Moans and groans echoed around the room until I felt her vagina walls began to pulsate, squeezing my fingers. I could tell that she was climaxing. Her aggressive rocks transformed into an uncontrollable spasm before she collapsed on top of me. As she laid there, capturing her breath, I couldn't help but plant sweet kisses on her inner thighs. I could feel her cheeks rising as my kissing sensation transported through her body.

After a moment of composure, I began to feel the gentle trace of her tongue between my clitoris and Nelson's shaft. Smirks wide, my vagina began to voluntarily arch towards her mouth, causing a more intense grind between Nelson and I. But the licks caused him to thrust harder and harder in search for the next. The harder he thrusted, the louder I groaned. I could feel my lady walls holding onto his penis, lingering on to the sensation. The tight grip caused him to swell inside of me. His penis inflated to almost treble its original size before finally ejaculating. "Aahhh… Raven…" he uttered as his eyes twirled back in his head. His whole body stayed tense for a short while as he jerked out his climax. Then, he ejected his penis almost immediately before fastening his robe. Void hollowed and dripping wet. My legs laid there limp, too exhausted to move.

"Thanks," Mara whispered before climbing off of me yet I was too tired to respond. Only my eyes had the strength to watch her as she vanished through the door and down the hall. My eyes smiled at Nelson as he covered my decency and left a kiss on my forehead.

"Goodnight, my beautiful black bird," he breathed before closing the door behind him and leaving me all alone. Too tired to think, I turned to the side to relax my heavy eyelids.

~ Chapter 19 ~

The next morning, I rose to the sound of reggae music penetrating the air waves as the bright sunlight penetrated my eyelids even more so. My body began to turn underneath the Egyptian cotton as I tried to readjust myself. I could smell the nostalgic fragrance of fried dumplings and fried plantain which woke my stomach up but my mind still felt exhausted. I laid there for a while; collecting my thoughts whilst my vagina throbbed. It felt like a swollen pulse was squeezing through my canal making me slightly uncomfortable. Though my memory of the night before was slightly hazy, the soreness confirmed my thoughts. I had done the dirty with him last night, in his house. My mind woke up at the thought of it and a flush of embarrassment clouded my cheeks. Images of Mara kissing me flashed through my mind. *Was she there too?* I wondered. The healthy hangover had altered my memory and somehow I was unsure of all of the details. For a while, I tried to piece the puzzle together but there were still huge chunks missing. The pink glow from the sunlight lingered over my eyes until I finally decided to open them and figure out what had happened.

Sweet Love blazed out of the stereo in the kitchen. I began to smile to myself with one eyebrow raised slightly as my mind drifted back to my night shift. I contemplated on how coincidental it was that this song of all songs was playing as I rose up out of my sleep. I pulled back the covers to head to the bathroom. My entire body ached. It felt as though I had done a full body workout at the gym. Nonetheless, I trudged to the bathroom to give myself a once over. It wasn't the prettiest sight I had seen in the mirror but I had to make do. I decided to freshen up with some soap and water so that I looked half decent then I redressed myself with the clothes I had worn the night before.

I headed down the swirling staircase and into the dining room. The help were busy cleaning the hallways as I sauntered down. They greeted me politely as they passed me by. As I walked through the double doors, I saw Mara already seated at the dining room table, looking as fresh-faced as ever. Her soft curls held that just-washed look as they bounced off of her jaw line. Her eyes still sparkled as bright as her teeth and her freckled skin still glowed. I was stunned. I didn't understand how she woke up like this; flawless. Looking as good as her upon waking was only a figment of my imagination.

"Good morning, Raven. Did you sleep well last night?" She smiled at me audaciously.
"Yeah. I had a good sleep thank you, though I am still a little tired. You?" I responded politely as a great yawn left my mouth.
"Of course. I always make sure that I get a good night's sleep and a good coffee gives me the morning boost that I need." Mara laughed and I joined in cordially.
"Where's Nelson?" I questioned in wonder.
"Oh, he's having a lie-in. He was absolutely exhausted after last night plus he needs to take all the rest he can get in his condition." She squinted at me playfully. I wasn't surprised that he was exhausted as I felt the same. I stared at her for a while, unsure how to respond. I wasn't sure how much she knew about last night but she didn't seem to be giving much away. "You must be famished. Help yourself to some breakfast." She gestured to the abundance of food on the table. Fried plantain, fried dumpling, breadfruit, boiled banana, boiled yam, ackee and salt fish. It was a feast for the eyes let alone the stomach. She was right, I was absolutely famished and in need of some food to wake me up properly. Without hesitation, I reached for the serving spoon to fill my plate with all of the breakfast delights.
"Thank you," I said as I began stuffing my face. "This tastes delicious!" Though my fingers ached, I barely seemed to notice the pain as I devoured every morsel of food on my plate.
Mara began to smirk. "So I take it you have enjoyed your stay here then?"

"Yes. It's been lovely and that Egyptian cotton feels like heaven!" I replied.

"We've enjoyed having you here. I must say, I did particularly enjoy those kisses on my thighs. It was a nice touch." She winked as she spoke and my eyes widened in shock. I knew it. I knew she was there last night as well. Parts of my memory seemed too lucid for it to be just a dream. I began to smirk. "I can tell you are good with your mouth." She stared into me as she spoke and my face flushed hot. It was not even noon and she was already dishing out the hors d'oeuvres.

"Likewise." I grinned as the memory of her tongue on my clitoris came flashing back like a Polaroid camera. "I've never experienced anything like that before, you know, with a female," I shared slightly embarrassed to say it all out loud.

"Trust me, some of your best times will be with a female. We know what we want and we know how to give it, if you know what I mean." She gazed into my eyes. Her look made me feel awkward, still flustered by it all.

"Really? So you've done this before with a girl?" I questioned her, intrigued.

"Of course! Nelson brings the girls here all time. That guest room has seen many o' female but I must admit, you are one of the best," she sneered as my stomach almost swallowed my Adam's apple. I was in disbelief by her words.

"What do you mean?" I needed some clarification.

"That hotel he works in is just full of girls who are just gagging to sleep with him. And I let him as long as he brings them back here. It's part of our arrangement," she said casually.

"Arrangement?" My blood began to boil as I swallowed her words. I knew they were open but this took the biscuit. This wasn't the arrangement that Nelson told me about, in fact, I'm sure he told me that his wife was none the wiser.

"Yes. You didn't think you were special did you? You're just another notch on our very expensive bedpost! "She cackled. My stomach was full of anger at the audacity of her and the deceit of Nelson. *Another notch on our very expensive bedpost;* the words rang in my ears. My eyebrows scraped my forehead line in search of the piss that she was taking out of me.

"Right, I see," I responded in a dignified manner, though I was raging inside.

"I'm sure those sheets will be dry cleaned by next week and another bitch will be rolling around with us in that bed," she brazenly added. I was stunned; this time in disgust. I was so taken aback by her words that I couldn't find my own. I sat for a moment. The taste of crisp fried dumpling dissolved into a puffy mush as it sat in my mouth. I wretched internally. I had suddenly lost my appetite.

"Well ... thank you for the breakfast but I am completely stuffed." It was clear that I had bitten off more than I could chew. "If you'll excuse me, I'm going to head upstairs to get the rest of my things," I finished as I edged away from the table.

"A taxi will be down stairs for you in five minutes," she called as I exited the dining room.

My eye's rolled aggressively though I knew not to act out of turn. I was in unfamiliar country in an even more unfamiliar side of town; I had no intentions of doing anything that I would later regret. My teeth gritted as I went back to the guest room. As I looked around, I couldn't help but imagine all of the guests that had been in that room. Strong visions of girls laughing and moaning as Mara slowly seduced them with Nelson cultivated in my mind. I could see his buttocks bouncing on top of legs that spread like butter. I could see Mara rubbing her tongue all over those unsuspecting girls' bodies. My stomach hurtled into my throat. I quickly gathered my things and headed to the front door. I couldn't stand to be in that guest room any longer.

As I walked down the stairs, I could see Mara waiting for me in the front foyer. I forced a smile as I headed towards her though I was close to cursing the life out of her. She bit her lip as I got closer, I could see her undressing me with her eyeballs and I almost felt naked. *How dare she?* I thought as I crossed my arms across my bosoms in an attempt to cover my modesty. Though I was already fully clothed, somehow, it made me feel better.
"Thank you for coming, Raven. It was a pleasure." Mara extended her hand towards me as though we were closing a deal.
"Likewise." I nodded in her direction as I walked through front door. I couldn't bear to touch her again.

"I'm sure Nelson sends his love!" she called out as I walked down her steps and my skin grew cold. The sound of his name made me feel numb; lifeless. I barely turned back to acknowledge her remark.

The taxi doors closed behind me and my eyes began to well up. *How could he do this to me?* I felt used. My thoughts travelled back to the times he had spoken about his wife and the way he had made it seem. Every time he spoke about her, he was adamant that she was none the wiser. Every time he spoke to me, he made me feel like I was the most important woman in the world. *Why would he invest the time to lie to me?* I couldn't get my head around it. A single tear rolled down my cheek as I tried to come to terms with it all. I had been deceived and it was a hard pill to swallow.

~ Chapter 20 ~

I could barely open my puffy lids the next day. The tiresome tears made my eyelids heavy and heart ache. A grey cloud sat above my head yet the sun shone on. I tried to carry on with normal activities though I was lost in my thoughts. My mind was clouded with regret. I regretted believing him, fucking him and finger fucking her. All I wanted was a bit of fun and he had ruined it with his lies. I tried to enjoy the poolside cocktails but they left a bitter taste in my mouth. Even the Jerk burger at The Jerk Hut didn't taste the same. It tasted bland and made my tongue dry. Everywhere I went, it reminded me of him; I couldn't even bring myself to say his name. It made me feel sick to the stomach. I had a few missed calls from him but I refused to respond. I refused to be lured back in with his excuses. I wanted nothing more than to get out of the hotel and see fresh sights.

After a long and hard battle with my mind, I headed to the excursion desk to find out what was happening in the day. I was in need of something new and exciting to lift my spirits and take my mind off of things. Behind the desk, sat a short and stocky middle-aged man. He wore a blue cap, though we were inside and a striped polo shirt that was so tight that it hugged his moobs as they hung over his stomach. I could tell that he enjoyed a hearty meal or two. His full beard was shaved clean though a tuft of coiled hair sat on his chest in between his unbuttoned collar. Sweat droplets formed on his nose and seemed to multiply as I approached him.

"Good morning ma'am. How may I help you?" he asked before I had even sat down. He had an uncontrollable smile and a keen glint in his eye.

"Hi, I was looking for something fun to do today and I was wondering what excursions you had on offer?" I spoke as I got comfortable on the seat.

"Well, there's quite a few things going on today but what is your idea of fun?" His eyebrow rose. My eyes squinted slightly as I tried to figure out whether he was flirting with me or just being friendly.

"What do you mean?" I quizzed him.

"Well, would you like to be entertained or would you prefer to take part in an activity?" He licked his lips. My nostrils began to flare. I was almost sure that he was flirting with me but not sure enough to set him straight.

"I think I would prefer some entertainment today," I replied straight-faced, upholding the highest level of professionality. I was in no mood to be wooed by a man who was almost the age of my father.

"Okay. I think I have something in mind for you…" he paused, " It's a mixture of both so you can decide whether you want to be entertained or whether you want to take part." My eyebrows raised slightly, I was intrigued to hear what was on offer. "There is a bus leaving for Negril in the next 30 minutes and they are taking persons to the cliffs for some diving."

"Diving?" My eyes bulged out of their sockets.

"Yes ma'am. Some like to climb the cliff and dive into the water. It's a big tourist attraction out here. But like I said, you can go and watch. You don't have to take part." He chuckled.

"I see. How much is it?" I asked inquisitively.

"Well, it depends. If you take the bus it will cost $50 but if you go with me it will be free," he said with a smirk on his face. My lips pursed at the audacity of him. I was now 100% sure that the comments he was making were more than customer service but I refused to entertain his advances.

"I think I'd prefer to take the bus but $50 sounds expensive. Is there no other way of getting a discount?"

"Well, if you are refusing my free offer then I suppose there's not much I can do. That price includes travel, tour guide and unlimited food and drinks. It's a good deal." He tried to convince me.

"For $50 dollars? That sounds a bit extortionate!" I fired back. "What about without the unlimited food and drinks?" I asked curiously.

"Without the unlimited food and drinks it will cost you $35 ma'am," he responded and my eyes lit up.

"Now that sounds more like it. You should've told me that price before! What time will the bus be here?"
"The first bus arrives at 11.30 am and leaves Negril at 6.30 pm. It's about 2 hour drive ma'am," he responded and my smile grew even wider. It was the perfect escape for the day. I gave the clerk my details and waited by the bar in the lobby for my bus to arrive.

* * *

After a long and bumpy ride, we arrived in Negril alongside the wide-stretching cliffs. The bus parked outside a cafe that was local to the cliffs and we all climbed out of the vehicle. A wave of music blasted through the cafe and the locals sang along to every tune. High-rising rocks spread along the seabed that surrounded the cafe and a few people played in the sea below. Flights of stairs travelled from the sea all the way up past the cafe and onto the sky-high landings. Wooden posts elevated out of the highest points of the cliffs to create extended levels of diving for the thrill seekers. I certainly wasn't one of them. The thought alone of being extended into the air sent shockwaves through my body.

Upon arrival, we were greeted with a complimentary drink from one of the lovely hostesses that worked at the café, even though she knew I that wasn't eligible for unlimited drinks. I could tell that she was skilled in the art of schmoozing as she worked her way through the crowd. She led us to an outdoor area which was home to an Olympic sized pool. Couples gathered by the pool bar as the waiters attended to their orders and the divers attended to the cliffs. I sat on the edge of the pool in search of the best view of the cliff diving show. From where I was sat, my eyes had access to all viewpoints; from the baby cliff edges to the extreme. As my feet dangled, I exhaled at the relief of it all. It felt amazing to be in a new environment with new people.

Whilst I sipped, I watched as the tourists and locals climbed and dived into the ocean below. My heart pounded a little faster almost every time someone took a leap of faith off of the edge.
"Woii! You are a sight for sore eyes!" A voice came from behind and as I looked up, my eyes gleamed in surprise as I embraced the mutual feeling. His tight top sat well around his chunky muscles and his bright eyes shined in my direction.
"Junior!" I called out, slightly elated. "I could say the same about you! What are you doing around these sides?" I asked as he perched himself beside me.
"I came down to visit a few friends, they are over by the cliff. But I noticed you from a mile away so I had to come and say hi." My eyebrow rose in suspicion. It had been almost a week since I had spoken to him and I honestly thought that he had forgotten about me.
"But you don't know how to respond to my messages though?" I jived though I had hardly noticed until now.
"My schedule has been back to back until now, you know with performances and ting. And I suppose I didn't want to keep

disturbing you on your vacation." His excuses were weak but I didn't care. I was just glad to bump into a familiar face that wasn't from *The Vacation Lodge.*

"Why would you think that you would be disturbing me?" I asked out of curiosity.

"I don't know. It just seemed like every time I tried to talk to you, you seemed distracted." His hazel eyes looked slightly solemn. Though his suspicions were true to a certain extent, I casually shrugged them off.

"No not at all. I'm on holiday to get to know people and have fun. I'm open to talking to anyone really." And I was now more open than ever to meeting new people and getting over him.

"Anyone?" His top lip rose to one side.

"Well, not anyone but decent-looking people," I clarified.

"So, am I decent-looking enough?" He nudged me playfully. Though I didn't mean it in that way, I jovially eyed him up and down for good measure.

"I suppose you can pass." I began to smirk as he embraced my sarcasm. "So are any of you guys cliff diving today then?"

"Yes of course. I get paid to do things like this!" he boasted and I speculated whether he was slightly exaggerating the situation. "I'm climbing up in a minute, are you coming to watch?"

"Yeah, why not?" I eagerly replied. Seeing Junior make a dive for it was something worth watching.

Strips of water dripped off of his legs as he climbed up onto his feet. He lowered his hand towards me to support as I climbed out of the pool and I followed him as he trekked to the highest point on the cliff. A few people noticed him as he walked to the top and stopped him to say hello. And I forgot how different it was being with him; he was like a local celebrity. Every time someone came over, I took a step back so that they could have their time. Though I enjoyed the V.I.P treatment when I was with him, I considered whether the constant stopping for random people was something that I could get used to. Soon we were well out of reach of the cafe. My heart pounded harder with every step that we took above the cafe grounds. The further we travelled up, the smaller the people got and the more I started rethinking my decision.

"Are you sure it's safe?" I asked for reassurance.

"Of course. I've been doing this for years and nothing hasn't happened to me yet." He shrugged off my worries. "Stick by me and you'll be fine."

Bars barricaded the cliff edge where the audience watched and I happily went to join them. The climbing had taken the breath out of me and the air seemed to be thinner where we were. However, I wasn't actually sure whether the air really was thinner or whether it was just a figment of my imagination. The bars offered a level of safety that made me feel somewhat comfortable as I watched Junior continue up the wooden spokes that were elevated off of the cliff edge. As he reached the top, the MC announced his arrival, "Are you ready for the infamous Junior Hamilton?" he hollered down the microphone and the crowd cheered wildly. "I can't hear you? I said, ARE YOU READY for the INFAMOUS Junior Hamilton?" he repeated with even more volume and the crowd cheered even louder. It was a pleasant surprise to see how many people were interested in watching Junior dive.

As he stepped up to the board, he began to introduce himself to the crowd which caused them to get even wilder. His chants and dances amped them up as he gave them a show stopping build up. He reached for the branches above him for balance and began to levitate his legs off of the board. His abdominals tensed as he straddled his legs and brought them towards his body. The distance between my eyebrows and lips increased in amazement; I was quite impressed by not only his strength but his flexibility. His dreads dangled wildly as he manipulated his body into a variety of positions. My eyes were fixed on him, anticipating his next move. As he lowered his legs, he began to balance with one hand then the other when the MC boomed, "Alright ladies and gentleman, I want you to give a massive countdown from 10 for Mr Hamilton. Are you ready?"

"10, 9, 8…" the crowd chanted and my perspiration rate doubled. As soon as they had reached zero, he leapt into a backflip off of the ledge and shot down into the sea below. My heart collapsed for a moment or two as I watched. A mighty splash lurched into the air as his body catapulted under water. The crowd roared and I stood frozen, waiting to see if he was okay.

Moments later, his head bobbed back up to the surface and sense of relief swept through me. He began to shake off his locks and he trudged through the water. Then he looked up in my direction. I could see his gap-toothed smile as clear as day from where I was standing and I rushed down to meet him at the tidemark.

"That was amazing what you just did there!" I said in utter astonishment when I reached the last step.

"Really? That's nothing. I do this all the while," he breathed heavily.

"Well, you're a braver person than I am!"

"Well, it doesn't take much to be braver than you now does it?" he joked and we laughed together. It was such a relief to be smiling again. "So what are you doing later?" he asked as we sat on the rocks.

"Nothing. I'm just taking it easy today," I mentioned, knowing that my sole intention was to get over the trauma and disrespect that I had endured.

"So, why don't you roll with me tonight? We're going to a hotspot down here in Negril," he openly offered but I couldn't possibly attend.

"Negril? No I can't do that! My bus is leaving at half 6!"

"So… You know if you're with me you're going to get home safely." He spread his arms wide and I thought for a moment. I was unsure. I didn't want to be stranded in Negril. I began to think of a suitable excuse.

"I don't even have a change of clothes or anything. I think I'll give that one a miss."

"Oh, come on, don't be a spoil sport. How often are we both in Negril together?" He tried to convince me but my mind was already made up.

"No, not this time but I'm sure we can meet up soon."

"Alright. Well, I'm back in Montego Bay tomorrow. Can I take you out then?" he offered quite eagerly and that sounded ideal. It seemed much safer to be out in Montego Bay rather than in Negril.

"Yeah sure. Just let me know where and when." He smiled as I accepted his offer and I was grateful to have something to look forward to.

~ Chapter 21 ~

I noticed that something was different about me as I got ready to meet Junior. My cheeks were glowing and it wasn't because of my ridiculously expensive highlighter brush; though it did help. I had a spring in my step. Though I was still hurting slightly, I was ready to move on and let go of the drama that came with Nelson. He had tried to call me a few times but I was adamant not to pick up. I had no intentions of hearing his pitiful stories. Junior gave me a new lease of life and something to look forward to. Junior wasn't my usual type but he was easy on the eye. Either way, it was nice to have some company in the evenings. I only had a few more days left on the island and I wanted to make them count.

It was nearing 7, the time we had arranged to meet, so I only had time to put on my finishing touches. I wore a skin-tight mini dress with wedged heels and a dangling gold necklace that reached right down to my stomach. I spritz my skin with my favourite perfume which made me smell absolutely appetizing. My chest rose as I looked myself in the mirror; it was amazing what a good lick of makeup could do. I felt sexy again. As I left my room, I sent Junior a quick text to let him know that I was on my way then I headed for the lobby.

My hips swung like a pendulum as I walked to the front gates causing my dress to rise up my thighs. I could feel the security guard eyeing me up as I walked by but I paid him no mind. I tried to re-adjust my dress classily as I walked in the attempt to not reveal too much of me. Not all attention was good attention. I pulled out my phone to see if he had seen my message and he had. Though he hadn't replied, I knew it wouldn't have been long before he came rolling around the corner. I stood idle for while looking towards the end of the road. Five minutes passed, then ten but still, there was no Junior. As I waited, my feet began to ache. I had been standing on the street corner for more than I had bargained for and he still hadn't turned up. I began to grow worried. I deliberated whether I had gotten the time wrong or whether he had forgotten. I scrolled down my phone in search for his number.

Ring.
Ring.
Ring.

There was a pause. "*We're sorry, but the number you have dialled is currently unavailable. Please try again later.*" I exhaled a short huff. *Where on earth was he?* I thought to myself. *Why was his phone currently unavailable?* I looked back through my phone to confirm our meeting time. I was right. It was seven. But it was past seven and he was nowhere to be seen. I mulled over the possibility that he was running on Jamaican time but my feet were too tired withstand the waiting.

"Where are you?" I messaged as I walked back towards to sofas in the lobby. I waited for a while to see if he would read my message but he didn't. He hadn't been online for a while.

"Are we still on for tonight?" I wrote soon after for clarification. There was nothing more that I couldn't stand than waiting but I gave him the benefit of the doubt.

"Would you like a drink ma'am?" a passing waiter offered. He could tell I was waiting and I had been for a while.

"Sure. Can I have a Strawberry Daiquiri please?" I ordered in a pursuit to bide my time.

"No problem ma'am," he said as he left me politely.

A few moments later, the lovely, young man appeared with my Daiquiri in hand. I began to sip slowly as I waited for Junior to reply. As I sat, I saw groups of tourists queue, hop on and off the mini buses. Once. Twice. My eyes wound back in my head the third time I saw the mini bus pull up. *Where was he?* I was being extremely patient with him; more patient than I was used to. I had been waiting for almost an hour. I searched through my phone once more. He had read my message. Then my eyes lit up as he began to type.

"Sorry love. I got caught up in a session. Come and meet me. I'll send you the address." My lip pursed as I read the message. Though part of me was annoyed at him, I was relieved that he had finally replied to my message. I was all dressed up and wanted somewhere to go. I only would have been spiting myself if I declined his offer. I replied in haste to find out the address and began to head there.

* * *

Within 20 minutes, my taxi had pulled up outside the old park in town where he had asked to meet. The sky had transformed from purple to black with only a few stars twinkling in the night sky. As I stepped out of the taxi, I scanned the streets for Junior. But the night mist made it hard for me to see anything clearly. Only a few street lights were scattered along the road side and the cars were few and far between.

"Yo! Raven!" A voice hollered from down the road. When I looked in the direction of the voice, I could see the shadow of him, waving enthusiastically as he staggered towards me.

"Where have you been all my life?" he joked as he closed the distance between us. I raised one brow as I glared over to him but he didn't seem to take it seriously. Clearly my "not impressed" look was not convincing enough for him.

"Where have you been, more to the point?" I fired back as I eyed his stagger. He seemed to be in jollier mood than I was.

"I've been here waiting for you," he joked as he grabbed me by the waist. As he leaned in, I could smell the booze on his breath and it explained his unbalanced stance. He had a glazed look in his eyes and inerasable smile.

“I can tell you’ve had a few," I commented as I leaned my head slightly away from his.

“A few what?” He sniggered.

“Drinks?” I added.

“Yeah. A few of the boys bought some bottles to our session. I think that’s why time ran away from me. Sorry baby.” He winked as he finished. And for some reason, I felt a slight rush underneath my skin as I processed what he was saying. *Baby?* I hadn’t been called that in a while. There was something about the term baby that made me feel so infantile and submissive.

“It’s cool. I’m over it now," I replied feeling in a slightly more forgiving mood. “So, where are your friends now?” I changed the subject.

“Oh, they’re still in the park. Come. I want you to meet them," he said as he lured me in the direction of the park entrance and I happily followed. I was keen to see who he was with and meet some fresh faces.

Darkness fell from the sky and swept across the entire park making me feel slightly blind. My awareness heightened. Though it was not an easy task, my eyelids stretched further apart to refocus. I suddenly became sensitive to all that surrounded me. I latched onto Junior’s arm as he led us through the lengthy grass. I could barely see a thing and he was my only sense of support as we ventured through. Above the rhythmic sound of rubbing crickets was dull beat of musical merriment in the distance which grew stronger as we walked closer to it. The thick grass brushed past my toes as I steadied my clumsy steps. Between Junior's stagger and my steps, I was hardly sure who was supporting who.

The strums of guitars and the beat of the drums became much more vivid as we neared the logs in the centre of the park. I saw a small group of guys rapping and chanting to the rhythm of the sound. As our figures became clearer to them, I could make out the bright smiles on their faces. Junior began to slap hands with them all as we entered to circle of logs. He introduced me to every single member of the group and great smile smeared across my face as they all embraced me. I couldn't help but notice that I was the only female in the middle of a pitch-black park. I hoped that my smile was convincing enough for me to seem easy about the situation. My mind raced for a moment, worried about how safe I was but all the talking and laughing put my mind at ease and lightened my paranoia.

Junior handed me a bottle of tonic wine to drink as I sat on one of the logs. I sipped slowly as I nodded my head in time with the hooking vibes that they were creating. He reached for another stout and ripped the bottle cap open with his bare teeth. As he took a few swigs, he sat close to me on the log, making it clear to all that I was with him. Though I found it slightly funny, it made me feel warm inside that he was marking his territory; it was quite endearing. One wine turned into two then three, giving me a whole new feeling of park vibes. I had never been to a session quite like it before but it was quite the unique experience watching live talent only metres away. I could feel Junior glaring at me for a while before placing his hand around my waist. I found it a little odd that he was glaring at me so obviously but I gave no attention to it. I took it as a compliment that he was taking the time to admire my beauty.

"You look so damn good you know," he whispered in my ear whilst his friend rapped. I couldn't help but giggle. The passion behind his words was compelling.
"Really now?" I goaded him in search for more compliments.

"Of course. How can you not know how good you look? That dress fits you well and hugs you in the right places…" he added as he placed a light squeeze on my buttocks. My eyes closed involuntarily as I savoured the moment. I could feel the buzz in my cheeks as I smiled internally.
"Thank you," I replied in a dignified manner. As I peered over to him, his hazel eyes stared deep into mine.

"Come nuh. I wanna talk to you," he softly demanded as he began to get up from his seat. He leant his hand towards me in the aid of helping me up. I smiled as I rose up out of my seat and pulled my dress down.
"You need help with that?" he cheekily asked.

"No. I think I can manage," I responded almost automatically though I enjoyed his forward humour.

He grabbed me by the waist as he led us away from his friends and up the hill.
"What did you want to talk about?" I asked as we clambered into the darkness.
"Me and you?" He smirked and I exchanged a similar look back in his direction.

"What about me and you?" I eyed him from the side trying to hide my expression.
"I wondered whether there could be an us?" he asked and my eyes shot over to him. I had only met up with him a few times so was hardly expecting this sort of proposal.
"An us? Maybe... if you played your cards right," I brashly replied and he paused for a moment. I could almost hear his brain ticking over as he scanned my whole anatomy.

"Well right now, I have a royal flush," he breathed as he grabbed me from behind and pressed his piece firmly on my bottom. Right there and then, it was confirmed that he well and truly possessed a royal flush. As the sensation raced through my veins, I began to giggle timidly. Forest of trees crowded over us and dimmed the natural light that came from the stars. We were so far away that his friends were now the size of miniature figurines and the rubbing crickets over powered their music.

His warm mouth began tasting the back of my neck; avidly kissing and biting as he rubbed his hands all over my stomach then my breasts.

"I've been dying to have you all night…" he whispered as grinded his hips into my behind in a rhythmic fashion. My eyes began to close once more as he nibbled the back of my shoulders.
"Mmm…" I breathed automatically as his fingers cupped over my breasts. My head leant back towards him almost instantly.

"I know you like that…" he rasped as he spun me around. He began backing me into the shrubbery as our tongues intertwined with each other. It felt electric. My fingers slipped through the back of his locks as my tongue lapped his. He gripped my body with dominion and it made me want to submit to him. The meat of my behind placed firmly into his hands whilst my tongue explored his tonsils. My head swirled as he impressed passionate kisses down my front.

As his mouth explored my chest, my hands began to climb down his back and into his trousers. I clenched his firm behind tighter as the diameter of his mouth stayed vacuumed over my bosom. Blood rushed to his suction, forming a deep, purple impression on my chest. My eyes widened as I had realised what he had done to me.

"You're naughty…" I chuckled as my teeth clenched onto my bottom lip.

"Of course. And I wouldn't have it any other way…" he said as he fingered a handful of my derriere. He urged his body close to mine once more. He was rock solid. I could feel the length of him through his jeans as his wood rubbed between my legs and his hands caressed my behind.
The more he rubbed, the higher my dress rose above my bottom, slowly revealing my thong line.

As my hands traced his back, I felt him release my bottom cheeks. I could hear the struggle of him removing his belt buckle and unbuttoning his trousers. My head moved back from his.

"What are you doing?" I asked in the hope that he would audit his actions.
"What do you mean? I want to feel you closer to me," he breathed as he revealed his underwear. I flushed hot with bother. His jeans sat closely underneath his bottom but neither my body nor my mind were ready for that.

"I can't…" I murmured as I hung my head low. Though I enjoyed our kiss, I wasn't ready to open up in that way after the way Nelson had made me feel.

"Of course you can. I've seen the way you've been all over me." His lip rose to one side as he spoke, half revealing his gapped tooth. He pulled me in closer to him slathering his penis onto my crutch. A strange sensation came all over me. I could tell that he was ready but I knew that it wouldn't feel right having another man inside of me.

"Sorry Junior but that's not what I want right now. I'm up for fun but not that type of fun," I explained and he backed his head away from me to eye me up and down.

"You're kidding me right?" He sniggered as he held my head through his hands. "You think you can get me this hard and not finish me off?" As he spoke, he grabbed my behind and pressed my hips into his gear stick. "I know you can't say no to this." He grunted as he rubbed his cock aggressively on my knickers. My body began to stiffen. I sized him up wondering whether he was serious or not. My eyes followed his movements as he persisted to rub over me.

"No Junior," I said bluntly as I pushed his chest away from mine but he pulled me towards him with more force. My heart paused momentarily as my eyes quickly scanned my surroundings. The trees crowded over us and the shadows from the bushes were closing in on me. The intermittent rustle coming from behind me seemed to grow louder. It was just the two of us. In the dark. I could feel my vagina seizing up.

"Stop playing with me," he badgered as he slurped his tongue through the centre of my bosoms. I felt my heart plunge through my chest. I grabbed hold of his head but he only pressed down with more force. "I know you want me as much as I want you," he breathed down my neck as he coerced me to the ground. As I backed away from him, he held me tighter, pressing his fingers deeply into the small of my back. His sharp claws pierced through my skin as I tried to elbow him off of me.

My heart pounded with more force as I struggled to stay upright. My eyes rapidly followed my racing thoughts. *He wasn't going to? He couldn't.* My mind battled with my reality. Despite my attempts to resist, his strength over powered mine as he wrestled me down. "No I don't! Stop!" I barked with more urgency but he ignored my demands.

Stumps of soil jumped up hastily as my body collided with the floor below me. Neck high in the air, I tried to use my arms to push myself away from him. But the more I pushed away, the more he pulled me towards him as though it was a sick game of cat and mouse. Trickles of sweat began to drip from my forehead.

Why wasn't he listening? I thought. I began to retch at the thought of him. He began to drive my clammy thighs away from each other to nestle his way in but I was determined to keep my knees together. He gripped into them more aggressively, causing a deep indent where his fingers plunged.

Though I fought tirelessly, he forced my legs apart with the weight of his torso. My legs became weak as did my might. As he towered over me, his lengthy dreadlocks dangled over my face.

He grinned at me as I struggled, holding me down by the neck. The force of his grip made it hard for me breath.
"Please! Stop!" I gasped as my legs scrambled around his. As he held me down, he began reaching for his dick through the fly of his boxers.

"You think you can say no to this? Again?" he scoured as he rubbed his bare cock over my clitoris. "I know you like that!" He grinned as he watched my eyes well up.

"Please!" I begged as he continued to grind his penis over my vagina. Tears streamed down my face as I struggled to get away from him but his strength was more than I could manage. My vagina began to moisten the more he rubbed himself on me but my mouth was drier than the Sahara desert.

"You see… I knew you wanted it!" he huffed as he shifted his penis to my vagina hole.
"No! Stop!" I pleaded. My hands scrambled across the ground below.

Bang!

Bang!

Bang!

The jagged rock catapulted at full force into his forehead. With every hit, my teeth gritted as I struck him with more might than the last. He stopped mid-motion.
"Aaargh!" he grunted as he reached for his forehead. His grip around my neck weakened.

Bang!

One final blow from the rock forced him off of me. Blood gushed violently from his head as he whimpered on the ground. My eyes widened. My heart raced. I rushed to my feet.

Stomp!

His dick squelched as my thick wedge drove through his bare scrotum.
"Aarghh!" he yelped in the highest of pitches.
"No means No! Dickhead!" I howled as I stomped through his privacy once more.

I scurried to fix my dress before racing through the park. My breathing quickened the more I pounced down the hill. Wind blew ferociously past my face and the bushes rustled in the darkness. Wells of tears blurred my vision but I raced at full speed towards the entrance. I couldn't believe that he had actually tried to violate me. I looked behind me momentarily to see if he was there but he was nowhere to be seen. Just a sea of blackness. As I looked forward, I stumbled over my ankles and fell to my knees. My bones jolted as they shattered against the ground. A strong heat raced through me. I yelled in frustration. Only the comfort of my hands broke my fall when they shot out in front of me. A gash of blood dripped out of my calf as I struggled to my feet. I had been scraped by the bark of a tree but I didn't care. All I wanted to do was get out of there. I wanted to be out of the park and out of his sight.

As I continued, I ran back past the logs and the benches in centre of the park. The logs were silent. There was no one to be seen. For a moment, I questioned where his friends had gone and whether they were watching me. In reality, I had no time to worry about anyone but myself. My heart grew heavy and tired but I was determined. In the distance, I could see the opening of the black gate onto the street. My legs powered through the long grass leaves. I wiped my face as I ran to clear my eye site and my makeup smudged all down my hands. I couldn't believe that I had went back there. I should have known.

Finally, my eyes lit up as I reached the gates and bolted straight out. I took one final look behind me to see if he was near but he wasn't and I exhaled a sigh of relief. Though the streams of tears rolled down my face incessantly, I was glad to be away from him. *Why me?* I asked myself as I sought for the street lights but I couldn't find an answer. I only hoped that I could find myself safely back at the hotel.

As I continued, my legs ran out of steam and turned to jelly. The blood had begun to dry on my calf and my feet slowed as I reached the infamous strip. The frequency of lamp posts had doubled and the visibility of life tripled as I neared the fast food restaurants. My face fell solemn as I trudged down the road. Though I was grateful to be encountering more life forms, all I wanted was to find my way back to my hotel. I began to fix my dishevelled appearance as I neared the night life, wiping the smeared makeup from my face.

"Are you okay ma'am?" A car slowed beside me. As I turned, I was met with a heavy-set, dark toned man. He wore a thick, gold chain around his neck which matched the gold tooth in his mouth. Rings decorated his fingers as they clasped onto the steering wheel. He eyed me up and down for a while. Though he smiled at me, there was no hiding the concerned look that he had on his face.

"Yes. I'm fine." I forced a polite smile. I was in no mood to continue a lengthy exchange with another man.

"Are you sure? You look like you could do with some help." He took his foot off of the accelerator as he followed me along. I sighed heavily. Though I knew I needed help, I couldn't bring myself to trust him. His masses of gold just screamed that he used money for favours and that wasn't the kind of person I was trying to attract.

"Yes. Thanks," I shortly exchanged before placing my head forward. I had no intention of extending our conversation any further. I could still feel him crawling along beside me and offering more. My gut hurtled into my stomach. I didn't understand why some people found it so hard to accept someone's decline. I could feel my eyes welling up as the struggle I felt with Junior flashed back into my mind. I forced a smile and strapped up my armour. I didn't want him to see any weakness in me. I held my head strong as I paid him no attention and eventually he sped off. I relaxed my shoulders in relief.

By the entrance of *The Caribbean Cove*, I saw a female bouncer manning the doors. Her hair was shaved on both sides of her head leaving a strip of length down the middle. She had roughly scraped her curls into a top knot. Her layers of clothing were black and thick despite the evening heat that lurked in the air. I immediately headed in her direction. She seemed like the only person that I could approach.

"Please, I was wondering if you could help me?" I asked as I clasped my hands together in front of my chest. Her eyes began scanning me.

"Go ahead ma'am," she said as she attempted to asses my body language.

"Something terrible has happened and I'm trying to find my way back to my hotel." My Adam's apple began to swell as I spoke and her eyes weakened.

"What happened? Are you okay?" she asked as she searched my body with her eyes and my eyes began to well up. I was not okay. Involuntary shivers leapt through me causing my whole body to shake.

"I'll be fine but I just need to get back to my hotel. Could you please help me get a taxi?" On the street, I could see mobs of cars asking people if they needed a ride but my trust levels were low.

"Sure. No problem ma'am," she replied before having a quick word with her colleague. She unlatched the metal gate so that she could step out and began to reach in her pocket for her phone.

"Do you have money?" she asked before dialling the number. I managed to stable my nerves to search in my purse.

"Yes. I should have enough," I confirmed and she gave me a brief nod. She held a short conversation with someone on the phone before reassuring me that someone would be here to collect me soon. I grabbed hold of myself as I waited, trying to take charge of my shivers. I didn't understand where they had come from. It wasn't even cold.

Within a moment or two, a bright yellow seven-seater pulled up outside the nightclub with an illuminated taxi sign sitting on the roof. The red license plate was highlighted by the bright headlamps and was clear to read. I kept a mental note of it as the driver wound down his window. After all I had been through, I couldn't take any more risks. There was an elderly man in the driver's seat and he addressed the bouncer that waited with me by first name. She seemed familiar with him as she went over to the driver's window to have a chat before introducing me. Though his skin had lost its plumpness and his curls were turning silver, I could see a similarity in their eyes and the span of their noses.

"This is Blascell. He's going to make sure you get home safely." She smiled warmly as she supported me into the taxi.

"Thank you so much," I said as she shut the door behind me. The incessant shakes followed me in.

"Don't worry. You're safe with me. Where are you heading to?" he asked as I strapped myself up.

"*The Vacation Lodge*." I exhaled as I reclined into the seat.

~ Chapter 22 ~

Number blocked. I was done. I was done with the drama and hurt that came with men in Jamaica. *How could he?* A strong heat raced through my veins at the thought of it. I felt nauseous as I peered down to the deep purple bruises that were imprinted on my thighs. My lids closed in despair. Though I was sure that the physical scars would fade, I knew that a mental scar would be travelling back with me to London. I attempted to rationalise why he thought that it was okay to treat me in such a disrespectful manner. I was sure that I had made it clear that I wasn't interested but he kept on pursuing the situation. Perhaps I wasn't clear enough. The lump in my throat was hard to swallow. I relayed the whole night in my head over and over, wondering how I could have done things differently but it was too late. The damage was done. My entire body anchored into my mattress as I tried to readjust myself. Muscles that I never even knew existed ached in me and made my whole body feel sluggish.

Though I had slept for most of the day, my body still felt fatigued. It was the first time since I had been away that I had stayed in for the day but I needed it. I dozed in and out of consciousness as I watched repeats of *The Fresh Prince* and ate the crisps and chocolate that had been sitting in the mini fridge for over a week now. The food comforted me like a precious hug and dulled the memories of the night before though it felt like the most peculiar of groundhog days for me. Every time I woke up, I would feel fine then the pain would kick in and the memories would come flooding back. And as I ate and laughed along with the canned laughter on the sitcom, the memories would fade and I would fall asleep. Then it would happen all over again. Until my body couldn't handle the sleep any longer. The sleep paralysis had told me that enough was enough.

I shot up forcing myself to stay awake. After a long needed stretch, I sought to the minibar for the pain soothing drink that my body was craving. My lips pursed at the sight of the tonic wine that sat in between the prosecco and coke. The dreaded drink that he had coaxed me into having so that he could have his wicked way with me. Even though the alcohol percentage wasn't shockingly high, the aroma from the bottle brought back toxic memories from the night before so I opted for something less lethal to my recall. The bubbles fizzled in the glass as I poured the can of red bull into my generous serving of rum. My body eased in delight as I took the first sip. The rum and red bull numbed the pain but gave me the burst of energy that I needed.

My brain was alert and ready for stimulation. I no longer had any interest in the television and was bursting for some human interaction. I often felt like that when I spent the majority of the day to myself but the caffeine had heightened that need. I called down to the reception to book a reservation at the hotel's Chinese restaurant. Whilst I knew that I wouldn't be able to enjoy my evening meal with someone, I knew that some form of conversation would lessen my need to be stimulated. The evening was looming and I thought it would make a change to have something that wasn't "Caribbean" for dinner. I had just under an hour to get ready for my reservation so I slipped into the bathroom.

No more bikinis for me. I thought as I eyed myself in the mirror. Red raw cat scratches scraped across the small of my back and down the side of my calf. My attack was undeniable. My face dropped as I examined my body. I questioned whether the fun was worth it. Images of Junior's stares and hands all over me flashed into my head. I began to shudder at the thought of it. Barely being able to face myself in the mirror any longer, I hopped into the shower and gently soaped over my sore scars. I knew that I didn't have the confidence to reveal my bruises so I wrapped myself in a floor-length sheer kaftan. My insides squirmed slightly as I squeezed myself into my high waisted leggings. My muscles screamed internally as I tried to gently pull the tight fitting Lycra over my bruises. As I analysed myself, I could tell that my attire was no match for the weather. However,

I felt a lot more comfortable being wrapped up even though a warm heat still hovered outside.

As I approached the front desk of the restaurant, a very pregnant hostess greeted me. Her face looked swollen and tired and her stomach popped out from both sides of the desk. She was almost bursting out of her South-east Asian attire. I could tell that she had been on her feet for a while from the bulge around her ankles in her dolly shoes.
"Good evening. Welcome to our restaurant. How many persons will be needing a table?" she asked barely being able to make eye contact with me. I stared at her for a moment or two, slightly feeling sorry for her and her mouth hung open as she awaited my answer. Then her question registered.
"I just need a table for one," I politely replied, feeling almost embarrassed that I was dining alone. No matter how many times I had said the phrase "dinner for one," the embarrassment never faded.
"Sure. No problem ma'am. Follow me," she said casually shrugging off my concerns as though they were a usual request. For a split second, I deliberated whether it was normal to dine alone or whether she was too tired to care. Either way, she made me feel comfortable. She reached for a menu as she began to lead us into the main dining area.

A cool breeze of air conditioning embraced me as we walked through and the low-lighting in the restaurant created a calm and private ambience. The walls were a deep red and decorated with golden dragons and traditional black symbols. The soft sound of oriental music floated through the restaurant speakers in the corners of the room. There weren't many people in the restaurant when I arrived, just an older couple who sat by the window as they awaited their service. She led me to a table for two placed behind the pillar in one of the crevices of the room and handed me the menu. I liked where she had placed me. It was open enough to see the passers-by but closed enough for me to have some privacy. I exchanged a smile with her as I sat down to investigate the menu.

"Good evening, my name is Sasha and I will be your waitress for the evening. Would you like anything to drink?" A softly spoken voice came from above me and my eyes shot up, slightly startled by her presence. I had barely had a chance to sit down before another woman came to greet me.

"Erm, I think I'll just have a water for now," I responded hardly having the chance to look at the menu. She nodded as she walked away. Within seconds she arrived back at the table with a jug of ice-cold water. I sat back as she poured it into my glass. I could see that they were quick with their service at this restaurant. Though it wasn't as quick as selecting a meal at the buffet, it made a nice change to the Caribbean cuisine. I took while to scan the menu. There were so many appetizing choices that it made it hard to choose from.

"You haven't returned any of my calls." A deep voice hovered above me and I froze. Though a dark shadow towered over my table, I was petrified to look up. I had no intentions of seeing him or speaking to him ever.

"What on earth are you doing here?" I blurted out without a thought. My whole body went cold as my eyes met with his. Though I knew Nelson worked at the hotel, I was surprised to see him back here working; especially in this restaurant.

"They asked me to return to work but I wasn't ready to be on the main floor so they put me in here. Why have you been avoiding me?" he asked with a solemn look in his eyes and my own began to glaze over.

"You really have to ask me that?" I stared at him dead on as I spoke. The blood began to dart through me at double speed. Though the odds for seeing Nelson were not in my favour, I wasn't prepared for this. "Look, all I wanted to do was come out to have a nice evening meal and I didn't plan on having you spoil it." I huffed.

"The last thing I want to do is spoil your evening but I couldn't just stand up there and not talk to you. I've missed you." He spoke with a glint in his ebony eyes. My lids shut in an attempt not to hold eye contact for too long.

"Well, now is hardly the time. I'm in the process of ordering." I tried to keep the firm tone in my voice though it slightly touched a nerve to hear that he had missed me.

"What are you having?" he asked.

"I haven't decided yet!" I snapped back as I plunged myself into the menu.

"Well, I'd like to recommend either the sweet and sour prawn stir fry or the chicken in black bean sauce..." he paused for a moment. "Please allow me to be your waiter. I've spoken to Sasha and she doesn't mind swapping tables."

I squinted up towards him. "So, now you want to wait on me?"

"I'd rather wait on you than anyone else in the restaurant. Please. Don't make this more awkward than it needs to be," he spoke quietly. And as I looked up, I could see that Sasha had a close eye on our interaction. I decided not to make a scene any longer.

"Can I order the vegetable spring rolls and the sweet and sour prawn stir fry please?" I calmly requested. As he noted my order, he left my table with a nod. Behind my forced smile laid deep thought. *Why wouldn't he leave me alone? What did he want from me?* My head tried to trace his actions.

As I waited for my food, I could feel him hovering around me. Wiping tables that were already clean and fixing cutlery that was already straight. But he never said a word. He knew he was being watched by his staff members and he probably wanted to make a good impression since he had been off for a while. When my food was ready, he arrived at my table.

"Here you are." He smiled as he served my food on to the neatly spread table cloth in front of me. "Please give me a chance to talk to you." He locked into my eyes and my heart sunk into my chest.

"I don't know if I can..." I replied honestly. Seeing him again brought back all the feelings he stirred up inside of me and the deception felt raw.

"I don't even understand how things got like this so quickly but I want the chance to discuss this thing properly," he spoke low as he poured me another glass of water. His mind games were tiresome. He was trying to convince me that he didn't understand how things got like this and a small part of me wanted to believe him. "Please. You deserve it," he whispered as his blinking rate slowed. He placed my glass down and left without giving me a chance to answer.

As I ate, I thought. I considered how harmful it would be to my self-esteem talk to him once more and whether it was worth it; whether he was worth it. Though the food looked good, it was hard to enjoy when I had so much on my mind. The plump prawns swum in the sauce as my chopstick chased them around tirelessly. *You deserve it.* His words rung true. I did deserve answers but I could never be sure how honest he was going to be with me. He had convincing words but some of his actions didn't quite match up. I had been a victim to his sweet words before and wasn't willing to swallow another tough piece of humble pie. He had mostly been honest with me, but not always and that was the problem. I sucked the sauce off of the end of the spring roll that I had dipped in as I tried to come to a decision. As I attempted to enjoy my meal, I could feel him hovering over me; haunting me like the Ghost of Christmas Past. But I couldn't figure out whether his presence was a trick or a treat. My stir-fry grew cold as I sat and stared through the deep, red walls.

"Are you done with your meal?" he asked, stretching his hand towards my bowl.

"Yes. I'm stuffed," I mentioned as I sat back to allow him to clear the table. I lied. Though my stomach wasn't full, my mind was; full to the brim.

"You look beautiful tonight, by the way." His eyes shined as he watched me and I tried my hardest not to blush.

"Thanks." The taste of his words were sweet indeed but I was determined not to let him know that.

"Meet me at the Sports Bar. I get off at 10 tonight. I really want to talk things through with you," he continued as he stacked my used cutlery onto his foldable tray. My hollow eyes met with his as I listened to his words. "Give me a chance. Please," he urged before shuffling away from my table. My lashes locked slowly. I had a lot of thinking to do.

~ Chapter 23 ~

As the neon sign flashed before my eyes, I toyed with the idea of stepping inside. *Was it worth it?* I bit the peeling skin on my lips as I struggled to come to a decision. The movement inside was obscured by the tints on the window, yet as I stared in, I could clearly see the can of worms that were still crawling around from the last time I stepped through those double doors. So many questions inside of me longed to be answered and the more I tried to bolt that door shut, the more they tried to burst through the seams. My eyes darted back and forth as I thought. My chest froze, inflated with doubt. I couldn't do it. I turned the other way. But as I attempted to walk back to my room, my foot stayed firmly in place as though it was cemented to the ground. Internally, I battled with the idea of walking in and turning the other cheek. But something inside of me yearned for closure. With a huff, I exhaled the blast of air that I had been holding in whilst my eyes closed before me. *For the peace of mind alone*, I told myself as I plunged into the misty darkness that was the Sports

Bar. Clouded with confusion, I had no other choice but to convince myself of my words.

It was quiet; quieter than the last time I had been inside. A single member of staff stood behind the bar, shining glasses with his overused cloth. Flashes of light from the football match refracted on the tinted windows that surrounded the bar. The volume from the game was on low so the sounds of the glasses clinking on the table was clear to hear. From the back terrace, the dim smell of smoke floated into the Sports Bar, though it was not as pungent as before. And at the back of my throat, the stale taste from the sticky stir fry lingered like an unloved guest. Its presence had been heightened by my inhalation of the smoke that had wafted into the room. My tongue began to dry as it attempted to launch the unsavoury aroma against the roof of my mouth. In search of something strong enough to detox my taste buds, I headed straight over to the bar.

"Can I have a double shot of dark rum please?" I requested as I took a stool by the bar.
"Sure." The bar man nodded before turning to reach for the dark bottle of spirits. "Are you here alone tonight?" he asked as he poured a healthy portion of drink into my glass.
"Not really. I'm waiting for someone," I said before necking the entire shot in one gulp. My face winced at its bitter taste but it had cleared my throat somewhat. His eyebrows leaned towards mine.

"And you're in need of Dutch courage?" he probed. *Here we go*, I thought as I eyed his eager body language. It was obvious that he was bored and looking for a conversation. I cut him short. "Something like that," I bluntly replied before ordering another drink. I was in no mood for small talk. I had too much on my mind to digest before Nelson stepped through the doors.

In what seemed like seconds, he had concocted my second drink. I had been distracted by how I thought this evening would play out so I hadn't realised how swift he had been. As he poured the juice through the sieve, I could tell that the drink he made would not be as potent as the first. Before tasting my Mojito, I swished my straw around the crushed ice to analyse its consistency. I hoped it would be more consistent than Nelson had been as I took my first sip. The juice sat on my tongue momentarily as I savoured the bittersweet taste. Regrettably, it was more bitter than sweet. My lips pursed as I swallowed. I only longed for my conversation with Nelson to be more tasteful than my drink as I stepped away from the bar.

I sought rescue on a stool, in the corner, by one of the tinted windows whilst I waited. It was 5 past and I knew he would be walking through the doors anytime soon. My brain ticked over as I played out the conversation in my head. *Why did you lie to me about your wife? Why weren't you honest with me about your real arrangement?* I was ready to put him in the firing line and the dark rum shots had loosened me up. As I sucked on my mojito flavoured straw, I envisaged his responses. But nothing but invalid excuses came to mind; which slightly annoyed me. My eyes narrowed as I searched deeper for a convincing argument.

Moments later, the double doors swung open and Nelson waltzed in scanning the room for me. My heart began to pounce like a lion on his prey. I sat still, motionless as I waited for him to locate me. I had sobered up. Whilst a part of me wanted to blend into the background, hoping that he would never spot me, another part of me yearned to be seen and heard by him. He looked over by the pool tables then in the corner. There I was, drink in hand. My chest inflated once more. I tried to grab hold of my ever changing emotions as his eyes connected with mine but the struggle was undeniable. I was fucked. He saluted the bar man respectfully before closing in on me and my pre-game confidence began to waver.

"Hey!" He beamed as he leant in to embrace me but my body seized up. Though I had seen him coming, I wasn't ready for him. My conflicting emotions had me stuck. He paused as he sensed my dis-ease and then retreated into the seat beside me. "Were you waiting long?" he asked as he got comfortable on the seat.
"No, not too long…" I said as I sipped my bittersweet cocktail. He stared at me for a while as though he was waiting for me to add more but my mind had gone blank. An awkward silence darted back and forth between us as I searched for something useful to say.

Crickets croaked.

Glasses clinked.

Pool balls shot across the table beside us.

"What are you drinking?" he asked in an attempt to break the thickening silence.

"A mojito," I replied flatly.

"Oh, I love that drink. Do you want another one?" he offered.

"Sure. I don't mind," I said as I slurped between the crushed ice. "But with extra sugar please," I added in the hope that my next would be sweeter than the last and he smiled as he headed towards the bar. A breath of relief leapt out of me as he left the table. *What was wrong with me?* I wanted to get to the bottom of this issue yet I couldn't think of anything to say. I shook my head desperately in an attempt to focus my mind.

At the bar, I could see Nelson having a short conversation with the single member of staff that was working there. He had leaned in towards him, holding an interest in what he was saying. As they talked, my eyes focused on them, watching their every move. I was keen to know why the bar man had such an interest in what Nelson was saying and I wondered whether it was about me. Briefly, the bar man looked over in my direction and then nodded as he began to mix and pour the two mojitos into the glasses. My mind began to run into overtime the longer I eyed their movements. I had already felt uncomfortable and their conversation seemed a whole lot more interesting than ours had been. *Why on earth was he looking over at me?* I thought as they extended their engagement. Laughing wildly, Nelson grabbed the glasses and headed back in my direction. My lids narrowed as he neared me.

"What were you two talking about?" I asked before he even had the chance to sit down.

"Oh, I was just telling him about my injury because he was saying that he hasn't seen me around for a while," he replied casually and my brow began to raise to my hairline.

"So, why were you laughing?" I squinted as I awaited his response.

"He was just telling me not to get you too drunk!" He laughed as he relayed his message and I assessed his answer. "Paranoid much?" He smirked as he handed my drink to me.

"You can't be surprised can you?" I fired back and his eyes lowered in embarrassment.

"Don't be like that Raven. It's all love out here." The side of his lip raised as he spoke. His washed eyes looked up at me like a cowering puppy.

"All love? And was it all love when you lied to me about your wife?" My facial expression was as flat as my tone of voice. His chin shot up.

"Lied to you about my wife?" he said in surprise and my lashes tapered in an attempt to better read him. I couldn't risk the wool being pulled over my eyes again.

"Yes, about your arrangement. She told me all about it." I paused, waiting for him to fill in the gaps but he stayed silent. "...about how you sleep with girls and bring them back to sleep with your wife?" My eyebrow levitated towards him and his jaw hung low.

"She told you that?" he asked as his fingers began to trace his forehead. I couldn't make out whether he was confused or just in plain shock.

"Yes?" I asked with confirmation in my voice. "Is that right?"

"I can't believe that woman sometimes you know!" His hand began to tighten into a fist. It was clear that he was angered by this but I couldn't understand why. "She really said that?" he asked again.

"Yes… Is that right?" I looked into him harder and he refused to make eye contact as his eyes followed his thoughts.

"It's not like that and she knows it!" He huffed into his chest.

"What do you mean?" I questioned him for clarification.

"I don't just fuck girls and bring them back so she can fuck them too." His head hid in his shoulders.

"Oh, yes. I forgot about your *needs* like you conveniently forgot to mention your wife's *needs*." My disgust for him began to intensify as the image of him with his wife and the other girls resurfaced in my mind.

"No. It's not like that. You just don't understand..."

"So explain yourself then!" I snapped back before he could even finish.

"Yes, I do meet girls from time to time and we make a decent connection but it's her that wants to bring them home. Not me!" he tried to explain.

"Oh and I suppose that makes it okay does it?" I sharply responded.

"No, of course not but it's not my fault ..." One hand clasped the other as he urged for me to understand him but somehow, I couldn't quite get to grips with what he was telling me.

"Oh. So I suppose you accidently fall into pussy and conveniently invite that same pussy to come to your house?" His pitiful excuses were growing tiresome.

"No. We are in an open relationship but it's her that wants to sleep with girls that I meet." As he spoke, I stared at him in utter disbelief!

"What kind of sick game are you two playing? This isn't right!" My body began to stiffen. "I get that you work in a hotel. I get that you can get caught up sometimes but what I don't get is why you don't tell the truth about your wife? It's rude!" My face grew hot as my voice raised.

"Yes I know, it's a bit off-putting isn't it? But trust me if I had it my way, it wouldn't be like that." His eyes lowered in shame. *Off-putting?* It was more than off-putting to know about the possible amount of girls that had slept with him then his wife.

"If you had it your way? What exactly would it be like?" My mind struggled to come to terms with what he was saying.

"Mara has done a lot for me but sometimes she takes it too far," he continued and I almost spat out my mouthful of mojito as he tried to convince me.

"She takes it too far? You have control over what you are doing. Don't try and blame it on her." I refused to allow him to dodge responsibility for what he had done.

"No trust me, it's her. You think I want her to know who I'm sleeping with? You think I want Mara to sleep with who I'm sleeping with? No, that's not my style to be honest." He shook his head in disapproval and I could only stare at him in astonishment.

"I can't believe you! You misled me into coming to your house and you want to talk about style?" The blood raced underneath my skin.

"Trust me Raven. I like you. I never even wanted to bring you back there."

"If you liked me, you never would have Nelson." My thoughts slowed as I registered his words. Though I wanted to believe him, his actions confused the fuck out of me.

"I do like you but it's more complicated than you think. If I had it my way, I would leave her for you trust me but it's not as simple as that." He paused as though he was capturing his words before they left his mouth. So I waited silently to hear exactly what he was trying to say. "Mara is too much for me but I have committed to her so I have to stay." I gazed into him for a while. My mind closed in on his words. *He had to stay? What does that even mean?* I thought to myself as he sorrowfully hunched over his cocktail. I began to speculate whether he was spinning me another web of lies but his eyes looked weak and that mirrored in my heart.

"You don't have to stay if you don't want to." My tone softened.

"I do and I'm sorry. I really didn't want to hurt you." His lids closed slowly. Whilst it was hard to admit, a small piece of me had broken inside. And though my heart had grown fond of him, I knew it wouldn't last forever.

"I'm not begging you to be with me. I just wanted you to be honest with me." I held a brave tone as I swallowed my pain.

"I'm being as honest as I can. I'm sorry and I want to start a fresh with you." He reached his hand towards mine across the table. The stroke of his hand began to soothe my wounds.

"Listen, I'm going home the day after tomorrow and I'm not trying to leave the island with any bad blood. All I ever wanted is for you to be straight up," I told him as I gradually became accustomed to the touch of his hands over mine.

"I hear you." He nodded in agreement.

"I actually like you as a person but I can't deal with the lying." I laid my cards on the table.

"Neither can I. I'm sorry. Please forgive me, my little black bird." His ebony eyes met with mine and I began to swallow my pride.

"I'm over it but I just don't think it's a good idea for you to lie to girls about your situation." Though his lies still hurt, I stretched the truth a little.

"I'm sorry baby. Please let me make it up to you. I can't have you leaving this island mad at me. I really like you, you know." My heart opened as it longed to believe him.

"I don't live here. It doesn't matter to me but you can make it up to me if you want." I held up my facade though I was glad to hear his words.

“I have to. I want to take you out tomorrow," he insisted though I didn’t need much convincing to spend more time with him.

“If you want," I casually replied and he clasped my hands tighter as I accepted his request.

~ Chapter 24 ~

After a tight squeeze and a few shakes, my Pina Colada was ready and iced to perfection. As I grabbed the glass from the bar, I gleamed in delight, anticipating the sweet creaminess that I would devour in my first sip. Whilst I did love the taste, the feel of something in my hand gave me confidence and a distraction. Confidence in my actions and a distraction from my negative thoughts. The sun pounded through my skin, slowing my pace as I headed down the poolside steps. My only sense of rescue from the overpowering heatwave was the feel of the cool cocktail sliding down my throat. It was another sweltering day in Jamaica though the hue in the air felt somewhat different. The fog that clouded over my decisions gave me a sense of misdirection. *Should I really be doing this again?* I asked myself as my sheer black train followed behind my every footstep down to the beach. Though my mind told me to leave him alone, my heart longed to be with him once more. I took another sip from my deep glass of cocktail. *When would I get the chance to see him again after this?* My subconscious encouraged my footsteps. It was my last full day and I had convinced myself to live in the moment.

It was late afternoon yet the heat still thrived. I was in the perfect attire. My black, mid-thigh length, swimming costume sat well underneath my black sheer kaftan and hugged me in the right places. As my floor-length dress swiftly swept underneath my feet, sand smoothed across the floor behind me like a red carpet. Whilst the studded, V-neck dress neatly decorated the meat of my bosoms, it covered my bruised waist and wounded legs; that was the most important thing to me. I sought to the DJ booth, where we had agreed to meet, which was a few restaurants away. The beach was filled with young ones begging their parents to stay a little longer though their evening appetite was looming. Strips of seaweed brushed against the tidemark as the waves pushed them further into the sand yet the children didn't care. They hunted the beach for more; lining the motes of their sandcastles with the slimy, green wire. Above the sea, I noticed a flock of hovering gulls on the lookout for food though the majority of eaters had disappeared to their rooms. But I had a reason to be there and so did Nelson.

Speckles of sand vibrated underneath my feet as I neared the booth and the music roared across the beach. A small group were still gathered by the sound system enjoying the vibes that the DJ created. As I neared the booth, I could see that he was already there, all dressed in white. A flock of butterflies began to flutter in my stomach as though it was my first time meeting him. I knew it was my nerves. After all the time I had spent wondering whether I had made the right decision, it was too late. I was there. We were almost face to face. I took a sharp sip on my cocktail to balance my nerves. His contagious smile grew as he spotted me and I couldn't help but grow one on my own face. As I approached him, his knees began to bounce harder to sound of the music that leapt out of the speakers.

"The beautiful lady in black…" he greeted me with open arms and I felt a lot more receptive to him this time round. I inhaled deeply, relishing the moment. It felt good to be in his arms again.
"Hi. Have you been waiting long?" I asked as I embraced him.
"A little while but it's all good. The DJ has been keeping me company!" he jived as he gestured to the jockey that played above him. My eyes couldn't help but roll at his quirks. "I see you've come dressed for the occasion…" he smiled as he eyed my attire and I began to blush.
"Of course. I wouldn't have it any other way." I winked before burying my head in my shoulders. I couldn't quite figure out whether he was complimenting me or not but I never did know how to manage the spotlight gracefully.
"You look beautiful though, as always," he told me and the hairs on my cheeks began to stand on end; there was no denying that compliment.
"Thank you. And you're looking rather dapper yourself!" I replied in the attempt to take the spotlight off of me.

"Oh, this? It's just something I flung on!" he joked as he rubbished my comment. "So are you ready to jump aboard?" he asked as he signalled to the boat.
"Sure. Why not?" I responded in agreement. I figured it would be easier to converse away from all the noise and the people.
"Let's go!" He beckoned before reaching down to pick up an oversized basket.
"What's all this?" I asked as I tried to control my flaring nostrils.
"Oh, just a few bits and snacks for us," he casually replied and I began to smile as I remembered how thoughtful he could be.

The all-white boat bobbed by the shore as we walked right over. As we approached the boat, my eyes began to dilate at the sight of the glass bottom. The true depths of the sea could be seen beneath glass sheet that lined the bottom of the boat. My lips began to dry in the sweltering heat. The sight of wavering sea life beneath the foundation of the boat created an illusion of risk. It almost appeared as though I could drop right through the bottom of the boat at any moment. *How could this be safe?* I considered as I stared in. Before I knew it, Nelson had left me behind. Without a second thought, he had hopped right in causing a sudden jolt. Then he looked back at me, waiting for me to follow suit. I paused with an awkward smile smeared right across my face. His eyes rolled playfully before he grabbed me by the hand, guiding my wobbling feet.
"Don't worry. I got you," he reassured me after reading the terrified look on my face.

"I hope so." My awkward smile strengthened. The roof cascaded over the length of the boat, blocking the blaze of the sun, which gave me a sense of heat relief.

A stretch of bench seats marked the perimeter of the boat, allowing plenty of room to sit. Almost immediately, I perched my bottom on the deck seat, neatly tucking my feet behind so that they had zero contact with the glass bottom below. Somehow, I felt safer with my feet on the wooden slabs. "Relax. Nothing is going to happen to you," he said as he began unwinding the rope from the only piece of safety that held us onto the dry land. I looked around hastily for more security.

"Aren't you going to wait for the captain?" I queried as he confidently loosened the slacks.

"I am the captain!" He laughed as he chucked the rope into the boat.

"You mean to tell me you are going to drive this?" I questioned him shock.

"Yes. Don't you know I'm a Jack of all trades?" His chest rose in pride, as did my eyebrows.

"You never told me you own a boat!" I gazed up at him rather impressed and he chuckled at my ignorance.

"I don't! It's my father's but he taught me how to drive it," he casually shared with me. "Come to the front with me and I can show you the ropes," he said as he extended his hands towards me.

"I can't…" I fearfully murmured

"Don't be silly. Of course you can!" he goaded as he grabbed hold of my hand to pull me to the front. I reluctantly followed behind. As he escorted me to the bow, he ushered me in front of him. "You know how to drive don't you?" he confirmed as he placed my hands on the big, black wheel and I nodded in agreement. "Well, there's hardly any difference!" he exclaimed as he fired up the engine and a strong base of music bolted out of the boat stereos.

The sound system was as strong as the turmoil of the engines. A thick, white whirl of foam formulated in the sea around us as the boat took off and he immediately placed his hands on top of mine. I could feel his strong presence behind me as the wind brushed past my face; arousing safety inside of me. The bow rose above the waves and the boat sped up fiercely but his expertise allowed him to get everything under control. My eyes began to water at the feel of the fresh sea air rushing past my face, slightly blurring my vision, so he assisted in putting my rose- tinted glasses on. As he fiddled with the technical buttons, he allowed me to steer for a while. The pressure around my shoulders began to ease as I got used to the motions on the boat and soon we were far away from the shore. I began to embrace the cool air as we drove into the distance.

"I want to take you somewhere," he said as he took control of the wheel and steered us in a whole new direction. Waves splashed violently as he turned us around.

"Where are you taking me to?" I asked inquisitively.
"It's a surprise." He winked as his secretive eyes slit over to me and I began to glow internally with anticipation. My chest bounced buoyantly as the boat mounted the waves and sprinkles of water sprayed against my face as he teared through the ocean.

It wasn't long before he slowed down and switched off the roaring engine. We began to float aimlessly in a vast stretch of deep, blue drift.
"This is where you wanted to take me?" I tried to mask my unimpressed look.
"Yes. Come here," he urged as he pulled me by the hand. Below my feet, sat a glowing coral reef through the glass bottom. My eyes gazed in amazement. Countless numbers of colourful fish rushed past as the glass magnified their movements. Then a party of large turtles swam below, almost stroking the bottom of the boat. I was mesmerised.
"Wow! They are beautiful!" I exclaimed.
"I know, right?" His head rose in glory for a moment. "Do you want to jump in?" he asked and my breathing halted for a second.
"Erm...I'm not sure." I struggled for words.
"Why are you such a coward all of the time?" he mocked me jovially. "Nothing's going to happen to you! I've been here hundreds of times with my dad," he told me in his most convincing tone but the fear kept me rigid.
"But I'm not that strong of a swimmer. What if I drown?" I tried to think of an excuse.

"In this shallow piece of water? I doubt it. Besides, there's life jackets on this boat so you can easily just jump back in when you're ready." I could tell that he wasn't going to take no for an answer. "C'mon don't be a spoil sport!" he said as he began stripping down to his swim shorts and strapped a bright orange life jacket around him. "I even have these…" he mentioned as he pulled out a pair of snorkels from his giant basket.

"Wow! You really came prepared. Didn't you?" I said as an uncontrollable smirk began to grow on my face. I had always wanted to snorkel but had never been in the position to.

"Of course! Come on, I know you want to." His ebony eyes glistened against the water as he placed the snorkels on his head.

"Alright! I'll give it a go…" I reluctantly told him and he began to gleam at his successful attempt of twisting my arm. As he reached for my sheer kaftan, my muscles began to solidify in embarrassment. He began to pull the dress over my head and I knew what was coming next.

"What happened to your leg?" he inquired as his finger traced the perimeter of my wound in a concerned manner. A flash of Junior's force shot into my head but with a strong blink or two, I managed to bat away the thought of him. I delayed in answering as I searched for a suitable excuse but nothing fitting came to mind.

"Oh, I fell over the other night and scraped my leg! It's massive isn't it?" I exclaimed as I joined in with just as much concern. I figured that if I couldn't beat him, I may as well join him.

"Yes. You look cut real bad but a bit of sea water will cure that bad boy in no time!" he reassured me.
"I hope so. It's looking real ugly," I said as I gently inspected the wound along with him.
"Of course. The sea water is the best cure for those sorts of things," he mentioned as he buckled up my life jacket. "So what are you waiting for?" he asked before diving right in. A tornado of back splash splattered all over me as he landed in the water, freezing what was left of my bravery. He swam over to me as I sat on the edge, dangling my feet in the water. It wasn't long before he lifted me up off of the edge and launched me right in. My body shivered relentlessly as it acclimatised to the cool, blue water then he dragged me along as we dived below the surface.

As my eyes adjusted, I noticed the sea was illuminated with bright, glowing colours. Underwater flowers bloomed and swayed in time with the waves whilst the creatures of sea ducked in and out of them. The focus on my breathing intensified as I blew big bubbles through the water. Thankfully, the life jacket kept me afloat as I delved deeper into the sea world. Scuttles of fish rushed between my legs as we swam by in search of the party of turtles. A group of them gathered by the reef as they sought for some food. As we got closer, Nelson leapt forward to grab one and I leapt back in uncertainty. But he stayed cool, rising the turtle to surface of the water. "Touch it," he urged as he placed my hand on the hard, slimy shell. Though I was slightly afraid at first, I quickly got used to the leathery feel of the sea creature underneath my palms. I embraced the feeling for a moment before he released the turtle back into the deep ocean. I watched in awe as it swam back underneath the water and I began to smile at Nelson. "You see it wasn't that bad," he told me as he placed his fingers through mine and planted a salty kiss on my lips.

After we had explored the ocean, we travelled back towards the drifting boat to jump aboard. My limbs felt heavy as I climbed onto the boat and my eyes felt tired. Sensing my exhaustion, Nelson placed a warm towel around me and began stroking my arms. It didn't take long for me to grow accustomed to being in his arms once more. For a while, we sat on the glass bottom boat and relaxed as it bobbed over the calm waves. The sun transformed from a bright yellow into a fiery red as it reached horizon and a rosy mist spread across the ocean then the sky. He reached into his basket and pulled out some foil parcels for me. I was curious to see what was inside. When I unwrapped the foil, it revealed a healthy piece of Jerk chicken and crisp fried dumplings; my eyes beamed in delight. I welcomed the smell for a moment, relishing in the fact that it was still warm. The swimming had exhausted me and worked up an appetite inside of me so I was excited to tuck in. Jerk sauce dripped down my fingers as I devoured my chicken thighs. To savour every last taste of the meat, I placed my fingers deep into my mouth before mopping up the excess sauce with my sweet, fluffed dumpling. I was so overwhelmed in satisfaction that my stomach swelled in delight. Moments later, he reached into his basket once more;

this time revealing a bottle of wine which poured as red as the ocean. Our eyes met as our glasses clinked and we began to sip slowly. The blood-thick liquid slipped right through me causing a pleasurable buzz in my system. I was on cloud nine.

"Thank you for giving me another chance," he said as he stared deep into my soul, igniting a fire that I thought had dimmed.

"It's my pleasure. I wouldn't have had it any other way." The wine began to talk for me. Whilst I knew I may have been at risk of oversharing, my cares slipped down the drain with every sip that I took. "I've never met anyone quite like you before. I'm going to miss you, you know," I divulged as I swivelled my lips around the glass.

"I'm going to miss you too, Raven. I never knew that you would make me feel like this but you have me thinking about you all the time." His eyes flirted with mine for a while making my heart swoop.

"I bet you say that to all the girls…" My eyes shifted to the back of my head as I tried to brush off his comment; though it did touch a soft spot.

"I don't actually. There's something different about you. You're not as airy fairy as the usual type of girl that goes for me. You are a real woman," he told me as he stroked his thumb over my palm. My eyes shut as smoothly as my inhale whilst I processed his words. *A real woman.* My inner goddess leapt for joy as I took it all in. "You have to keep in touch with me when you get back home," he pleaded.

"Of course, I will. As long as it doesn't cause any trouble," I said as I gazed back towards him.
"Trouble? You could never cause any trouble!" He began to chuckle at the thought of it and I joined in with him. My mind drifted to the day I would leave and a sadness grew inside of me. I let out a forceful huff.
"I'm going to miss this; laughing and joking with you." My eyes closed again, this time in despair as I imagined leaving him behind for England.

As my eyes began to resurface, I could feel the warmth of his breath encompassing me, his nose now brushing against mine.
"You can have me whenever you want me," he told me and my heart began to flutter. Our eyes met briefly before his dropped to my lips. I caught mine between my teeth hungrily as I anticipated his next move. My inner deity began to throb as his eyes moved from my lips to my eyes and then back again. I began to lick them apprehensively. I knew what he wanted and I wanted the same. Slowly my head began to rise towards his, brushing my lips against his. As our mouths connected, it truly ignited the fire that lived inside of me. That burning desire caught alight as his juicy lips pressed deeply into mine. My head rolled in delight. Without awareness, my hand began travelling up his arm to sculpt his head whilst our tongues intertwined with each other and our passion grew more intense.

He paused for a while as he admired my beauty and I began to shrink. I could feel the growing spotlight on me as I buried my head into my chest. Without a second thought, he cupped my chin with his finger as he began to raise it and eyed me once more. He smiled as he brushed his thumbs over my lips and a warm heat surged underneath my skin. I leant in towards him once more, this time with more urgency. Passion leapt through us as his chest rubbed against mine. Though we sat side by side, he urged his chest on top of mine whilst the crimson sun kissed the horizon. His hands began to run over my thighs and my bosom rose towards him. Tingles travelled through me as he reached towards my behind and I held him closer.

As his kisses trailed down my neck, my chin began to rise towards to roof of the boat and his hand crept up my waist. My eyes winced. A sharp pain leapt through me as his fingers trailed over Junior's mark. I tried to block it out as I smoothly adjusted his hands slightly further away from my ache. I wrapped my hands around him as he buried his head in my chest and began to smooth his lips over the meat of my bosoms. My eyes began to close. But as they closed, I could feel the wretched sensation of Junior hoovering over my breasts. I swallowed harder as the saliva built up at the back of my throat. Breathing sharply and deeply, I raised his head from my chest and pulled it towards my face. I pressed his lips deeply against mine as I worked harder to erase the image of Junior from my head. And his lips responded cordially, wrapping his tongue around mine as we exchanged juices.

As my shoulders relaxed, I began to exhale. Whilst our lip locking thrived, his hand began to search my torso and my hands followed in suit. He drew me in closer as my fingertips explored his back. His touch was light as it ran all over me then down by my pelvis. His breathing deepened as his thumb grabbed the meat of my inner thigh and I yelped internally. The delicate skin that encompassed the bruises on my thighs wept at the feel of him and my legs began to close. *What was wrong with me?* I thought as he continued kissing me. No matter how hard I tried to ignore the pain that Junior caused me, I just couldn't enjoy it. I couldn't enjoy him. A burst of images blasted into my mind of Junior grabbing me and groping me and grinding my neck to the ground. My eyes began to well up. I grabbed Nelson close. A single tear fell down my face as my cheeks rubbed against his and my heart began to pound.

"Can we stop?" I whispered into his ear as I held him close. His hands paused.

"Why, what's up?" he asked with a concern in his voice.

"I'm just not feeling it right now," I told him as I gently brushed my tear away.

"Did I do something wrong?" he queried with me as he backed his cheek away from mine to look me in the eye.

"No…" I paused as I tried to structure what I wanted to say, "I just don't want to rush into anything right now. Is that okay?" I confirmed as my cowering eyes looked up at him.

"Sure, no problem. I respect that," he said and automatically, I let out a sigh of relief.

"I'm sorry," I whispered as the guilt of under delivering ate away at me.

"You don't have to be sorry. Whatever you want to do, I'm happy with that." He consoled me with a firm rub against my arms.

"Can we head back to the shore?" I asked "I'm feeling a little tired." I was overwhelmed with exhaustion.

"Of course." He nodded in agreement as he wrapped the towel back around me and placed a kiss on my forehead. "Whatever you want," he repeated as he gave me one final look in my eyes and I began to smile.

It wasn't long before he had uprooted from his seat beside me and headed to the bow of the boat. He looked at me endearingly before firing up the roaring engine and heading back to shore. As the music blasted from the speakers, he lowered the volume and he peered back at me. It was at that point that I knew that Nelson was nothing like Junior.

~ Chapter 25 ~

"Stay with me," he begged as the taxi doors opened and I let out an endearing giggle. The driver had stepped out to launch my luggage into his saloon sized boot but I already had my hands tied.

"Now you know I can't do that," I told him as my eyes smiled wildly. As I looked up into his ebony eyes, I remembered the moment we first met; when his smile shined as bright as the sun by the pool. And now we were bidding our farewells. It was the last few moments that I would spend with Nelson and I intended on savouring every last bit of it.

"Yeah, I know you can't but I wish you could," he said as he wrapped both arms around my waist.

"Well, I'm sure there will be a next time," I told him as I wrapped my willing arms around his head and he paused.

"I hope so." He stared into me deeply before locking his longing lips with mine and I began to giggle like a schoolgirl.

"C'mon, we have to go!" I told Nelson as I peered over the to the taxi driver, "He's waiting for us!" After looking over to the driver himself, he could see that he was becoming restless. For a moment, Nelson eyed me up and down before biting his lip. I could tell that he wanted more of me but we didn't have the time. Irresistibly, he gave my bottom a cheeky squeeze and I tried my hardest not to enjoy his attention.

"No, seriously. Let's go now." My words contradicted my inner feelings as I grinned from ear to ear.

Eventually, I managed to unravel his hands from around me as I stepped into the taxi and he followed behind. We got comfortable in the back seat as he rested his arm around my shoulder and pulled me towards him.

"Where to?" The taxi man was finally able to ask.

"Sangster International," Nelson responded for me and I turned to him.

"You really didn't have to follow me to the airport you know." I said though I was grateful for the company.

"Of course I did. Who else is going to make sure you get off safely?" he turned to me with a fatherly brow. My eyeballs lifted slightly.

"I'm a big girl you know. I came here alone so I'm sure I'm capable of leaving alone."

"Yes, you came here alone and then you met me. So now it's my duty." He spoke with a noble tone and I shook my head at him mockingly.

"What are you? My knight in shining armour?" I held back my smirk.
"Well, if the cap fits…" his eyes slid over to me and my nostrils began to flare. I loved the fact that he always knew how to lighten the mood and that was something I most certainly was going to miss.

Just as I had gotten comfortable in his arms, I peered out of the window. A bright, blue sign stood before me. Sangster International Airport. It hadn't taken long to arrive and a great sadness grew inside of me. I knew it would take more than a few jokes to lift the heavy weight that was growing on my heart. I tried my hardest to suck it up. A few moments later, the driver pulled up to the drop off area and turned his engine off. No matter how hard I tried to ignore it, I could feel a sharp lump emerging in my throat. I watched the driver as he stepped out and began to retrieve my luggage from his saloon boot and I turned to Nelson.

"So, this is it." His sharp words intensified the pain in my throat and my eyes began to glaze over. My thoughts flashed back to our first drink, our first dance then our first date and my eyes began to overflow. I refused to accept that I wasn't going to be seeing him every day.
"Don't say that," I shook my head as the tears rolled down my cheeks. My reality was dawning on me and he began to smirk at me.

"Why are you crying?" he chuckled slightly.

"Because I'm going to miss this," I sobbed, "I never have this much fun in England."

My frown began to deepen as I stared up at him.

"Don't be silly. This isn't a goodbye. It's a see you later." He smiled as he wiped the tears from my face but as I smiled back, I knew my fantasy was over. I would go back to my reality and he would go back to his. I flung my arms around him tightly as I held him for the last time.

"I'm going to miss you," I whispered as my mouth brushed his ear.

"I'll miss you too." He spoke softly though he held me tightly. I gave him one final kiss. Though my salted tears dried on my lips, it was the sweetest kiss I had ever tasted. He pulled away while I was still in mid-flow. "Come on, you better go. I don't want you to miss your flight," he said as eyes flitted to his wrist watch.

"Okay." I nodded reluctantly before giving him one final squeeze. The taxi door opened. "Goodbye Nelson."

"See you later, Raven." He used his correcting tone and the door slammed shut behind me. I watched the car speed off as I walked into the airport and I knew that was it. It would be a long, lonely trip back to London and that was something that I had to mentally prepare for.

As I walked inside, a long queue stood before me at the check in. Everyone's smiles hung as low as mine and I knew the holiday blues were kicking in. An emptiness had emerged inside of me since I had departed from Nelson and the feeling seemed to be a common theme with those who stood before me.

The queue moved slowly as the staff traipsed through the customers and my stomach started to rumble. Though I hadn't eaten since I had woken up, I wasn't quite sure whether this new sensation had aroused to fill the growing emptiness inside of me. Either way, my desire for food had intensified but the queue still dragged. I looked over to the ladies that were manning the checkout stations. They moved like emotionless robots. They didn't seem to have an urgent bone in their body. I couldn't quite tell whether it was my growing hunger that created an illusion of slowness or whether they were, just in fact, slow. My patience began wane.

As I stood waiting, I thought long and hard about the sacrifices I would have to make. I was desperate to get through customs and security so that I could grab a bite to eat but time was not on my side.

When I finally reached the front desk, I pulled out my passport to hand to the lady and she began to size me up. I looked at her straight faced as she matched my face to my passport photo which was nearly a decade old. I had lost weight since then so the image was slightly outdated. I had been meaning to update it but never managed to get round to it so I was always barraged with a load of questions whenever I pulled my I.D. out. I tried to entertain her questions as quickly and politely as possible; eventually she accepted my bags and let me through.

But as I tried my hardest to breeze past customs, masses of people stood in front of me. I called to them politely as I tried to slither through but the majority of my requests were ignored. Everyone was in just as much hurry as I was though we slugged through the security systems. Tensions tightened in my shoulders as my impatience began to intensify.

As I looked at my watch I could see that time was running away from me but I was desperate to eat. Boarding had already started and I couldn't afford to miss my flight. I was due at work the next day and I knew that my boss wouldn't be best pleased if I didn't turn up. I thought quickly about the decision I was going to make. *Should I eat and be late or should I secure my flight and eat later?* I paced as I deliberated.

Sweat droplets formed on my upper lip as my feet picked up speed in the direction of the gates. But I had to get something. Quickly, I grabbed a bottle of water and headed over to the gates for boarding. I assumed that it would dampen my hunger until my next opportunity to eat. Within moments, I had ripped off the cap and began down the bottle as I marched on until I had finally reached the gates. Thankfully, my hunger had been masked and I had arrived on time.

My hand luggage bounced off of the cabin doors as I stepped inside. "Good afternoon and welcome to our airline." The lady in red greeted me with a plastic smile as I walked past her and I returned the favour. Though I had no interest in her and she had none in me, the forced greeting seemed to be aeroplane etiquette. The aisles were narrow yet the customers rushed on and the plane was filling up fast.

As I shuffled to my seat, I held my bag close to my back so that it did not bounce off of any more aircraft furniture or unsuspecting travellers. I scanned the aisles in search of my seat, *32 F,* as I tried to work my way past a small group that were loading their luggage into the overhead locker.

29, 30, 31…

Finally, I had found my row and I began to celebrate internally at the fact that I had managed to secure a window seat. I rejoiced knowing that I would have no one brushing past me or excusing themselves as they headed to the toilets. Though I would have to do the same to others occasionally, I would have peace and quiet.

As I arrived, I noticed a young man occupying the middle seat, *32E.* His business attire had caught my eye briefly as it stood out from the other casually dressed commuters. He wore a closely-fitted, grey suit with a maroon tie. And his bright, white shirt sat well underneath his blazer and over his built stature. His skin was a cinnamon brown and ran smoothly across his body which encompassed zero blemishes. A well-groomed stubble gathered by his upper lip and travelled down and around his chin, forming a perfect goatee over his strong jaw line. His square black frames sat over his tawny, brown eyes and rested on his broad yet refined nose. A dark Clark Kent sprang to mind. His hair was low and shaped sharply; I assumed he was coming from somewhere important or had somewhere important to be.

His eyes brightened as I approached him and he looked up at me eagerly as I spoke, "Sorry, can I squeeze past? That's my seat." I gestured to the window seat beside him as I smiled politely.
"Of course. Not a problem," he said as he pushed his sliding glasses back up his nose and rose to his feet. I paused for a moment as I registered his crisp and courteous voice; it felt strange to hear a British accent again. As he stepped out into the aisle, I acknowledged him with a nod and slid into my seat.
"Thanks." I exhaled as I rested my feet. I began to leaf through my bag for my shawl to keep me warm during the flight.

"So, did you enjoy your holiday?" he asked in an attempt to engage me in conversation. My thoughts wandered towards Nelson and my chest began to droop into the seat.

"Yes, but it was over too soon," I told him as I wrapped the shawl around me, "Yourself?" I responded cordially.

"It wasn't much of a holiday but it was nice to have a change of scenery." As he spoke, I nodded politely, waiting for him to finish. "My names Andrew," he continued as he extended his hand towards me.

"Nice to meet you." My etiquette smile had reappeared.

"What's your name?" he asked as he held onto my hand with a gentle grip.

"Raven," I replied as I withdrew my hand and placed it in my lap.

"Wow. That's an unusual name," he said in an attempt to re-open conversation but small talk made me feel uncomfortable.

"Thank you," I closed as I placed my headphones on to my head and turned my body towards the window. Though I had not turned on any music, there was nothing more awkward I could think of than trying to force conversation for more than ten hours straight. As I stared out of the window, I saw the sweaty workers loading all of the checked baggage onto the aircraft. And my eyes lowered in mourning at the not-so-subtle reminder that my trip was over.

I sought to my personal in-flight screen that had been placed on the chair in front of me as a source of distraction. As I scrolled through the countless movies and television series, I found it hard to find a suitable option. It was filled with shows that I had already seen and hardly any of the movies tickled my fancy. As I tried to come to a decision, my hunger pangs began to resurface.

Immediately, I pressed the button overhead to call a member of cabin crew to my assistance and it glowed. I reached for my water bottle once more as I strived to tackle my hunger.

"Would it be possible for me to get a packet of crisps?" I asked as soon as the woman approached me. My breath was hot and my mouth felt clammy so I took another swig from my bottle.
"Sure, no problem ma'am. We'll get everybody seated and I'll be right over," she assured me in her most pleasant of voices. I huffed as I curled back into my seat; I loathed the waiting game.
"I have a sweet, if you'd like one," Andrew offered after sensing my dis-ease.
"No, I'm good thank you," I declined knowing that if I'd accepted, it would only be inviting more awkward conversation with him. I shuffled through the films and settled on a movie that looked somewhat interesting *The Preacher's Wife.*

As the flight took off, I reclined in my seat and swallowed hard to unblock my muffled ears. It didn't take long for me to get into the movie as somehow, I found a strong relation to one of the main characters, though I had never been married. It was more her way of thinking that reflected mine. As I looked over, it seemed as though Andrew had found something to keep him occupied also. His eyes engaged as he leafed through a copy of *Men's Health* magazine. It didn't surprise me as I could tell through the bulges in his blazer that he looked after himself.

At the front of the aisle, I could see a couple members of the cabin crew occupying a trolley and my eyes lit up. Soon, it would be my turn to grab a bite to eat and I rejoiced in that fact. Although I knew that the trolleys didn't move as quickly as I would've liked them to. Waiting in anticipation, I kept one eye on the movie and the other eye on the loitering trolley.

Whilst I tried to keep myself distracted, the plane began to rumble quietly and the seat belt sign illuminated over my head. We had hit a slight spot of turbulence which caused a vibration underneath my seat. I reached for my seatbelt and strapped myself in as I waited for the trolley to come my way. But the trolley jolted forward causing one of the cabin crew ladies lose her balance. The second rumble was slightly stronger than the first. With this, I could see the ladies reversing up the aisle and back into their seat. My eyes locked into them. *What were they doing?* I huffed in frustration. But a violent shudder caused me to lose focus on them. The shudder was longer and stronger than before so I sat back in my seat as I waited for it to pass.

Kachoh

Kachoh

Kachoh.

The plane continued to quake. I waited patiently.

KachoH

KachOH

KacHOH!

But the longer I waited, the stronger it seemed to get. My heart began to pound through my chest. *What on earth was going on?* I thought to myself as my palpitations intensified. As I looked out of the window, I could see the wings of the plane trembling as they fought against the fierce winds. The plane rattled as it rocked from side to side. My eyes bulged out of my forehead whilst I tried to capture my paranoid thoughts and my fleeting breath. My pupils flitted from side to side as I assessed my surroundings. Then, darted around the plane.

Trapped in my seat by this damn seatbelt and this overhead light. I locked eyes with the other passengers. I longed to clarify my growing fears by the looks on everyone else's faces. Cheeks shuddered whilst people fiercely gripped onto the arms of their seats. Heads began to turn for reassurance. Patience was wearing thin.

An announcement came from the pilot, "We have hit some strong winds. Please remain seated as we try to recover. Thank you for your patience." *Strong winds?* It felt a lot worse than strong winds. Drinks spluttered onto the floor as they fell off of the unstowed tray tables. Bodies bounced from left to right as they strived to stay comfortable in their seats. My breath began to shorten. Panic swept through the entire plane as it began to stumble out of control. Passengers leapt for air as they were launched back into their seats. Then *oomph!* A fierce punch lurched me upwards and the pilot spoke again. "We are experiencing cabin decompression and we will have to perform an emergency landing." My heart lurched out of my chest. "Please place on the oxygen masks that are stored above your seats," she continued and my whole body froze.

Immediately, the oxygen masks fell from above us and dangled over my forehead. My lungs collapsed into my stomach. Andrews's hands rocked as he stumbled for his mask and he wrapped it round his face. But I was stuck, wheezing and gasping for air.

"Are you okay? Do you need help?" he asked as he turned towards me.

I tried to capture my breath.

"No... I'm okay.... I'm going... to be... okay," I wheezed as I tried to convince myself. As I went to move my stiff hands towards the mask, the aircraft quaked out of control. My hands were locked. And I was stuck in this damn seatbelt. Panic stricken. My chest rose and fell as I tried to stabilize my breathing.

Huuuhh whooo…

Huuuhh whooo…

Huuuhh whooo…

I tried again. With all of my might, I attempted to reach upwards but my arms wouldn't move. Paralysed. *Why me?* My brain struggled for answers. Sweat dripped from my forehead and my armpits began to clam up. I urged with all of my brain power but my hands wouldn't budge. My head felt light and dizzy. Tears rolled down my cheeks as my faint body crippled before my eyes. Depleted. Deflated. Defeated.

"Please let me help you!" Andrew begged with more urgency this time but I refused to show him my weakness.
"No... I am fine..." I rasped. Blood raced through my fingers then my toes. Then, it all stopped. A moment of peace swept through the plane and my pulse began to slow. Suddenly, eyes shot back, leaving only whites in vision. Lashes fluttered wildly while my head waved with the clouds. Then, a strike of bright light. A volt of convulsions jerked through my body, knocking my head on the chair in front and behind. My breathing rate quadrupled. Warm saliva dripped from my mouth as my chest ricocheted off of the seat. My legs jolted upwards and spasmed out of control. Heart blazing... Palms dripping... Eyes spinning... Blackness.

AUTHOR'S NOTES

How could it possibly end like this?
Find out what happens next in the second instalment of The Vacation Lodge.
Turn to the contact page to follow the author and keep up-to-date with the releases of all forth-coming novels.

ACKNOWLEDGEMENTS

First of all, I would like to thank my mother and father for encouraging me through every step and lesson in my life. My mother, for being proud of all of my achievements and showing support in all of my ventures no matter how bizarre they sounded to her. A big motivation for me was her constant obsession with hearing new snippets of my novel. And my father, for allowing me to follow in pursuit of happiness and having faith in every decision that I made no matter how whimsical it may have seemed. He has also acted as a rock in my lowest of times and I am eternally grateful for that.

Also, I would like to give thanks to my one and only sister Shay, who was selfless enough to offer her services as a proof reader of my novel of over 70,000 words. She worked efficiently to meet and respect my needs. And she was always available for critical advice throughout the writing process along with my cousin (my spirit sister) Nichole.

I would like to thank my cousin Kelly Nicholls who was the first to encourage me to transform my dreams from writing blogs into writing books as she embarked on her journey to publish her own book *My Favourite Bible Stories* for children of colour. Not only has she encouraged me but she has been a sounding board for advice and support in the publishing process and for that I am truly grateful.

Additionally, I would like to thank my partner Stefan, who has acted as a mentor and a muse throughout my entire writing journey. Not only has he willingly and unwillingly listened to parts of this novel and given me constructive feedback. But he has acted as a sounding board and inspiration for the creation of both the title and blurb of this book. Furthermore, he entrusted me with his camera in order to create an advert for The Vacation Lodge. And I'm thankful to his sister Kimberley, who stood in as a model for me also. I am truly grateful for the support both him and his family have offered me.

And I have truly appreciated the opinion of my beloved friends Melissa and Karena, who gave me initial feedback on my very first draft of chapter 1, which has changed so much since then. I am also grateful for the trusted opinion and constructive feedback of my dear friend Pinar throughout the development of my novel, front cover to back and my friends Laila, Kemi and Roxana and others for also giving advice, support and inspiration. And last but not least, I would like to thank all of my past employers for both consciously and subconsciously reminding me daily how important it was for me to complete this novel and share it with the world. For that, I am truly grateful.

ABOUT THE AUTHOR

Dionne Jennene Walters is a young, refreshing author's voice who was born and raised in South London, England. Studying at both City University and Goldsmiths University, she has achieved qualifications in Sociology, Criminology and Education. Her studies have helped her develop an intricate understanding of people, behaviour, motives and the way that we learn. As a young child, Walters always showed a strong interest in the performing arts and poetry. And her work as a teacher re-ignited her passion for performances and creative writing that had the ability to capture the audience's attention. Walters holds a strong belief in the power behind words. When they are used wisely, she believes words can excite, inspire and enable anyone to get whatever they desire in life.

CONTACT THE AUTHOR

Website: www.djwalterswriter.com

Instagram: djwalterswriter

Twitter: djwalterswriter

Email: djwalterswriter@gmail.com

Lightning Source UK Ltd.
Milton Keynes UK
UKOW04f2007190118
316485UK00001B/1/P

9 781999 927608